His quiet laugh sent goose bumps down the length of her spine. It wasn't a particularly comfortable feeling.

"Which question should I answer first?" he asked, amusement in his eyes. Yes, this was the Harve she remembered—but not a boy now, and therefore more dangerous.

"I'm here because I wanted to talk to you. The house was a logical place to look. I wanted to see if the rag-tag undersize brat who used to torment me was really this poised, confident woman."

He was talking about her childhood. Was it possible he didn't remember the summer when she'd made such a fool of herself over him?

"That was a long time ago. But you have to admit, even then I knew what I wanted." Suddenly realizing how he might take that, she felt herself flush.

"And you were never bashful about going after it." The amusement was in his voice now.

# ABOUT THE AUTHOR

Carol Duncan Perry writes about "strong determined women—heroines who recognize their hearts' desires and who are courageous enough to pursue their dreams." Women who are a lot like Carol, in fact.

Carol and her "personal hero"—husband Hubert—live in the Pacific Northwest with a cat of unspecified and undistinguished breeding.

## Books by Carol Duncan Perry

HARLEQUIN SUPERROMANCE
537—WINGS OF TIME
652—DANGEROUS TO LOVE

# THE PRODIGAL DAUGHTER

## Carol Duncan Perry

*Harlequin Books*

TORONTO • NEW YORK • LONDON
AMSTERDAM • PARIS • SYDNEY • HAMBURG
STOCKHOLM • ATHENS • TOKYO • MILAN
MADRID • WARSAW • BUDAPEST • AUCKLAND

ISBN 0-373-70775-4

THE PRODIGAL DAUGHTER

Copyright © 1998 by Carol S. Duncan.

# THE PRODIGAL
# DAUGHTER

# CHAPTER ONE

HARVE TREMAYNE was a practical man. He always considered facts and circumstances before deciding to act, and he never, ever, became involved in hopeless battles or lost causes.

Until now.

As he waited for the annual stockholders meeting of the Little Falls Community Bank to be called to order, he again examined possible options—and as before, found no solution.

Dammit, he'd known for years that unless the bank changed its ultraconservative practices, it was headed for trouble. In the world of modern finance the Little Falls Bank was an anachronism—a small private institution, wholly owned by descendants of its original founders. For more than 150 years the fortunes of the town and the bank had ebbed and flowed together.

Harve could almost feel Gideon Tremayne, his great-great grandfather and one of the bank's founders, glaring down at him from the larger-than-life oil portrait on the wall above the board table, his fierce ice blue Tremayne eyes demanding, *Do something!*

But what?

Numbers could sometimes be manipulated, but they never lied. As long as Cyrus Blackburn, the current bank president and chairman of the board, controlled sixty percent of the bank's stock, Harve was powerless.

What he needed was a miracle.

When the old Seth Thomas pendulum clock on the boardroom wall began to chime ten o'clock, Cyrus took his place at the head of the table. "As president of the Little Falls Community Bank..."

Harve paid only perfunctory attention to the chairman's opening remarks and instead, tried to formulate an argument that might make Cyrus listen to reason. He nearly failed to notice the sudden cessation of the old man's voice and the soft *whoosh* of the boardroom doors swinging open, then closed. Like everyone else in the room, he turned to see who was responsible for the interruption.

A woman, young and attractive, stood poised against the boardroom doors. She was slim and of average height, and dressed in a well-cut red business suit. Its severe lines failed to disguise her feminine curves.

There was something familiar about her, something... He frowned as an elusive image tugged at his memory.

Her simply styled dark hair curved gently against her jaw, emphasizing the determined thrust of her chin. Now where had he seen her?

"This is a private stockholders meeting," Cyrus said, his voice quivering with indignation.

"I'm well aware of that," the woman said as she stepped forward. "Don't you recognize your own niece? I'm Charlotte, Uncle Cyrus. Charlotte *Blackburn* Carlyle."

"Ch-Charlotte," Cyrus sputtered, the little color in his face draining away. "But...what are you doing here?"

"Surely you haven't forgotten, Uncle Cyrus—I celebrated my thirtieth birthday last week on April twelfth. Under the provisions of my grandfather's trust I, not you, now control the stock he left me. Probate on my mother's estate also closed last week, granting me the shares I inherited from her. I own thirty percent of the bank's stock. I've come home to claim my inheritance and, under the provisions of the charter, take my place as an officer of the bank."

*Charlotte Carlyle! Little Lottie Carlyle—all grown-up. Well, well.* Harve leaned back in his chair. It was true he'd hoped for a miracle, but he honestly hadn't expected to receive it. *Imagine that. A miracle in red.* His lips curved into a grin as he dismissed the inner voice warning him that Charlotte Carlyle was an unknown entity. He'd worry about that later. For now, it was enough to see old Cyrus squirm.

LOTTIE WATCHED her uncle's mouth open and close, then open again, as if he was trying to speak, but no sound issued from his mouth.

Her strategy had depended on surprise. If her uncle's reaction was any indication, she'd been successful. She resisted the urge to grin and felt the butterflies in her stomach settle to a quiet fluttering. Taking advantage of Cyrus's moment of confusion, she studied him.

The years since she'd last seen her uncle had not treated Cyrus well. He'd aged considerably; his gray hair was sparse and his sharp features seemed shrunken, giving him a bitter look.

The man on his right was her cousin, Jefferson Blackburn. A rounded, blurred edition of his father, he looked older than his thirty-eight years. On the other side of the table sat a strong-featured middle-aged man she recognized as board member Andrew Pettigrew.

Abigail Tremayne was seated directly opposite him. The Little Falls matriarch must have been nearly ninety, but unlike Uncle Cyrus, Abigail Tremayne didn't look a day older than the last time Lottie had seen her. Her still-thick snow-white hair was swept away from her face and restrained in a chignon low on the back of her head and her navy blue linen suit and ivory silk blouse bespoke wealth and respectability.

Lottie turned to the last man at the table, and as her gaze met his, she felt her already nervous stomach perform a long leisurely loop-de-loop. The only man in the room not wearing a traditional suit and tie, he was dressed in a cowboy's version of business attire: a pearl-snap shirt, string bolo tie and a cream-colored deep-yoked jacket. If he'd been standing, she was sure she'd see matching slim-legged trousers and polished cowboy boots.

He'd looked a lot younger the last time she'd seen him, but the famous Tremayne chin, with its deep cleft, was clearly identifiable. So were the bright blue eyes now examining her with curiosity. She had no doubt about his identity. He was Harvey Tremayne—Abigail's grandson, Little Falls's favorite son—and the man she'd foolishly once thought she loved.

As he boldly returned her scrutiny, her breath froze somewhere between her throat and her lungs. The intensity of his gaze set her hormones to fizzing like bubbles in a soda bottle. Fighting to ignore her disorientation, she jerked her attention back to the head of the table.

"But...but you can't do that," Cyrus said. Now his face turned a deep red.

"I assure you, I can." She was thankful her voice sounded strong and steady, even if her knees seemed ready to give out. She opened her portfolio and withdrew a sheaf of papers. "Documents filed at the county courthouse yesterday certify the closing of probate, the dissolution of the trust and a revocation of your power of proxy for the shares in question. I've made copies for each board member."

"This is preposterous!" Cyrus exclaimed. "You have no knowledge of the community or how this bank operates. You can't simply waltz in here and—"

Lottie shook her head and drew a deep breath. Her adrenaline high was beginning to fade. She should be enjoying this confrontation. Instead, she simply wanted it over. "You forget, Uncle, I have the blood of two banking families in my veins. My mother was a Blackburn and although my father wasn't a Little Falls native, the Carlyles are a respected Oklahoma banking family."

Like mist rising from the lake, silence again hung in the room, so complete, she could hear the rhythmic pulse of her blood. She kept her attention firmly fixed on her uncle, believing he would be the first to attack.

She was wrong.

"I'm surprised you refer to that," Jefferson said in a condescending voice, "considering that your father's..."

Indignation stiffened her spine. She glared at him, daring him to finish his sentence. Her cousin's voice faltered, then fell silent.

Lottie waited another moment before continuing, "I have an extensive banking education and several years of solid banking experience," she said, ignoring Jefferson's interruption. "I've attached a copy of my résumé to the papers I've just handed you. I assure you, I'm well qualified to join the bank's officers.''

"A résumé can be faked," Jefferson said belligerently.

"It also can be verified," she snapped back, "but for my purposes, it really doesn't matter."

She paused again, this time for effect. "Under the provisions of the original bank charter, the largest individual stockholder can automatically claim the position of chief executive officer. I'm willing to allow you to retain the title of president for now if you wish, Uncle Cyrus. Later, we'll see how things work out. Meanwhile please order my father's old office readied for me. I will report to work as the bank's new vice president next Monday morning."

She'd done it! Taken the bull by the horns. Thrown down the gauntlet. Twisted the tail of the tiger.

Lottie swallowed the giggle threatening to erupt from her throat. Heaven help her, she couldn't even think, except in clichés.

A quick inspection of the faces around the boardroom table confirmed the effect of her announcement. Time and motion seemed frozen in that exact instant between action and reaction. The look on her uncle's face wavered between fury and disbelief. Jefferson's expression was mutinous. Andrew Pettigrew looked pensive. There was a twitch to

Abigail Tremayne's lips as if she was restraining a smile.

And Harve Tremayne? His face was totally devoid of expression. In an earlier life he'd probably given lessons to a sphinx. Was he for her or against her?

"I'll grant that your thirty percent entitles you to a seat on the board, but the other stockholders may have something to say about you becoming a bank officer," her uncle protested.

"Charlotte has my vote," Abigail Tremayne announced. "That gives her the support of forty-five percent of the shares."

Lottie looked down the table to the elderly woman. Abigail returned her gaze with a twinkle in her eye and an expression Lottie could only compare to a magician who'd just pulled a rabbit out of the hat. Definite support there, but what about the other board members? Andrew Pettigrew? Harve? She could feel the latter's gaze on her face and again struggled to keep her composure.

"What about you, Andrew?" Cyrus asked.

"The bank's stagnating and I haven't heard you suggest anything that would turn it around," Andrew Pettigrew said quietly. "I'm inclined to go along with the little lady. I sure don't see the harm in letting her try."

"Thank you for your support, Mr. Pettigrew," Lottie said.

"You're welcome, ma'am, although as you

pointed out, you don't need it. It's all spelled out in the bank charter, exactly as you said. Cyrus has been using his proxies and the charter to hold on to his control of the board and the president's title for years, and he actually owns only fifteen percent. I reckon what's sauce for the goose is sauce for the gander. Or in this case, vice versa. I just want to be sure everyone understands my position.''

Cyrus frowned and, not bothering to poll Jefferson, directed his attention to the last man at the table.

''And you, Harve?'' her uncle asked in a voice that seemed as much plea as question. ''Are you going to let my niece, who hasn't stepped foot in Little Falls since she was a child, come in and take over like this?''

Lottie held her breath. She knew Harve held the key to her plans. If he opposed her, she might possess the title, but wielding the power and gaining the support of the community would be difficult. She'd made a fool of herself over him once, pursuing him with the single-minded intensity of a besotted teenager. Would he remember that infatuation? Could he forgive or forget the embarrassment that immature girl had caused him?

He seemed to hesitate for a moment, more for effect, Lottie thought, than because of indecision. Then he leaned forward in his chair. ''Well, Cyrus,'' he drawled, ''as Andrew pointed out, legally she's within her rights.''

His voice was rich and smooth, like velvet, but there was no misunderstanding the authority behind his words.

"I'll admit," he continued, "this has caught me by surprise. There's an old Latin maxim that warns 'Whatever you do, do cautiously, and look to the end.' Being a cautious man by nature, I think I'll abstain, but with her shares, plus approval from my grandmother and Andrew, she has the backing of the majority of the board."

Lottie knew she should be satisfied Harve hadn't opposed her, but couldn't help feeling somewhat disappointed. Didn't he realize she'd grown up, that she was no longer a spoiled little girl? Didn't he realize *any* adequate banker would be an improvement over Cyrus?

And she was more than adequate. She was damn good.

"It appears the bank has a new vice president," Abigail Tremayne declared. The satisfaction in her voice alleviated a little of Lottie's disappointment.

"Jefferson is the bank's vice president!" her uncle snapped.

"He can retain his title," Lottie answered. "It won't be the first time the bank has operated with two vice presidents. I believe you and my father once shared the position."

"You dare to mention your father..." Cyrus began.

Darn it, she *hadn't* intended to mention her father. Not again, anyway, but there was no backing down now. What had Cyrus done—erased William Carlyle's name from the bank's history? She doubted if the residents of Little Falls had such selective memories. In small towns old scandals were never completely forgotten.

Mentally she squared her shoulders. *Start as you intend to go,* she reminded herself.

"Oh, yes, I dare, Uncle Cyrus. I also dare you to make disparaging remarks about him. Good or bad, he was my father. Also be warned," she added, determined to put him on notice, "if we hope to keep the bank's doors open, the policies have to change."

She refused to flinch at the anger she saw in his eyes. "I'll welcome your cooperation, but with or without you, I'll do what's required to save the bank. If necessary, I'll exercise the power granted me under the charter to the fullest extent and regardless of my title."

"In other words, you intend to run the show," Jefferson muttered.

Her gaze swung to her cousin. "Exactly, Jefferson. I intend to run the show—beginning Monday morning."

Considering the rage she felt and the general tumult of her emotions, Lottie was thankful her voice hadn't yet betrayed her. She'd done what she'd planned to do—presented her case to her uncle and the rest of the board in a strong, forceful and professional manner. Bankers, she'd learned, especially female bankers, needed to be brisk and unemotional, or they ran the risk of being viewed as unbusinesslike and sentimental. Now she needed to get out of here without destroying that image or letting her anger show.

It wasn't running away, she told herself, only a tactical withdrawal. She might have won the first battle but knew the war was far from over.

"I'm sure you'll excuse me if I leave now. I have several things to do before reporting to work next week."

She glanced slowly around the table, making brief eye contact with each member of the board—until she came to Harve Tremayne. Determined to keep her expression under control, she faced him boldly. A spark of some unreadable emotion in his eyes again sent her pulse into double cadence. Feigning a calmness she didn't feel, she forced herself to hold his gaze for another moment before looking away.

"Thank you, Mrs. Tremayne, Mr. Pettigrew, for your support. Uncle Cyrus, Jefferson, I'll see you next Monday morning."

Hoping her trembling knees weren't obvious, she turned and, pushing open the doors, left the boardroom as abruptly as she'd entered.

## CHAPTER TWO

HARVE WATCHED Charlotte Carlyle exit the boardroom, her bright red suit almost as attention-grabbing as the slight sway of her hips and her long silk-clad legs. The combination was doing strange things to his libido.

Charlotte Carlyle! He shook his head, trying to reconcile his memories of a mischievous young Lottie with this poised, dark-haired woman.

He remembered her as a gangly kid with freckles, pigtails and perpetually scraped knees. She'd been impulsive and absolutely fearless, rushing headlong into any adventure.

He also remembered her as a winsome teenager who, one fateful summer, had pursued him with a determination that was both flattering and frightening.

He'd like to believe he'd resisted her neophyte attempts at seduction because of his principles, but if he was perfectly honest, it was probably youthful arrogance, not ethics, that had prevented him from succumbing to her charms. He'd considered himself an adult, a college man too sophisticated to take notice of a kid still in high school.

Did she remember that summer? Or had the events that followed overshadowed those halcyon days? When he'd returned to Little Falls during winter break, he'd found the community scandalized by the accusations of embezzlement against her father and his subsequent suicide. Lottie and her mother had already left Little Falls.

The woman who appeared before the board today had fulfilled the promise of beauty he'd seen in the young Lottie Carlyle. In the ensuing years she'd apparently learned discipline, too. She'd been cool, composed, controlled—far different from young Lottie's fools-rush-in approach to life.

And one look into the depths of her jade green eyes had made his blood sizzle.

He shifted uncomfortably in his seat, trying to convince himself this stirring of his hormones hadn't happened. Dammit, it shouldn't have happened. It was strictly an involuntary response, a biological reaction, like sap rising in the spring. She was no longer a naive sixteen-year-old, and he was certainly no longer the callow youth he'd been that long-ago summer.

Which made this attraction even more dangerous.

The sound of his grandmother's voice momentarily distracted him from his thoughts. "I doubt if Charlotte will be satisfied leaving the bank's reserve funds invested in those three percent bonds," Abigail told Cyrus.

"They're a solid no-risk investment," Cyrus said defensively.

Harve straightened in his chair, disgusted with Cyrus. The old man's banking philosophy was so conservative he pinched every dollar until the eagle squealed. That was the main reason the bank was in trouble.

Thank heaven, it was a moot point now. Surely Lottie would transfer those funds into higher-interest-paying accounts.

Wouldn't she?

She appeared to be a mature confident woman, but was she a competent banker? It was all well and good to celebrate Cyrus's downfall, but what if they were trading one incompetent for another?

Tuning out the discussion around him, Harve picked up Lottie's résumé and quickly scanned it. One entry in the employment history seemed to jump from the page. *Loan officer, Saint Louis Merchants Bank.*

His frown deepened into a scowl. Saint Louis Merchants—wasn't that the bank that had been taken over by a New York conglomerate last year? Hadn't the bank been overextended, its investment portfolio top-heavy in speculative ventures?

Lottie had appeared as if in answer to a prayer. Had his exhilaration over Cyrus's defeat deprived him of common sense? Experience had taught him that when something seemed too good to be true, it usually was.

He checked the dates on Lottie's résumé. She'd terminated employment at Saint Louis Merchants last year. Before or after the buyout? he wondered. At any rate it was obvious she'd been employed there for several years prior to the bank's landing in trouble.

As a loan officer, how much responsibility had she had for the bank's problems? Big-city banking schemes? Was that how she planned to turn the Little Falls Community Bank around?

No matter how pleased he was with Cyrus's no longer being at the helm, he couldn't help asking himself if the board had jumped too fast. What was that old English proverb? *Better the devil you know than the devil you don't.*

There was another scenario to consider, too. The acrimony between Lottie and her uncle was obvious. What if she'd returned to Little Falls for revenge? To destroy the bank and Cyrus as her father had been destroyed?

Okay, it was a possible motive, though not a likely one—at least not for the Lottie he'd once known. Still, he couldn't completely dismiss the idea. People did change. It'd been what? Twelve, no thirteen years since her father had died? What forces had shaped her personality since then?

Harve had assumed control of his inheritance at twenty-five, and he was proud of his success since then. In spite of dire warnings from his former trust officers, he'd taken his father's investment company public. Tremayne Diversified now boasted annual revenues that kept both him and his stockholders happy. And converting the home farm from a cattle ranch to a quarter-horse farm was also successful. The farm regularly grossed six figures and had an excellent reputation among horsemen.

Of all the holdings he'd inherited from his father, the bank was his only failure. And his greatest frustration.

Was Lottie Carlyle really the answer? Could she rescue the bank, put it back in the black?

Questions and more questions. He certainly wasn't going to find answers sitting here listening to Cyrus rant and rave.

He abruptly pushed his chair away from the table. "Grandmother, gentlemen," he said, "you'll have to excuse me. As always, when I'm not present, my grandmother acts as proxy for me." With that he strode from the room, leaving behind the surprised murmur of fellow board members.

As he exited the bank moments later, a quick look up and down the street told him he was too late. Sam Taylor's old hound dog sunning himself in front of the Down Home Café was the only sign of life on the deserted main drag.

How could she have disappeared so quickly? And where?

Ironic, he thought, that he was the one chasing her this time. Although he tried to tell himself it wasn't the same thing at all, the fine hairs on the

back of his neck prickled. He couldn't quite shake
the feeling that Lottie Carlyle was about to turn his
life upside down.

THE BUTTERFLIES were back. Delayed reaction,
Lottie told herself as she drove. Inwardly she might
be trembling, but the sensation was caused as much
by jubilation as anxiety. The board meeting had
gone according to plan.

Well, almost.

She'd known Cyrus and Jefferson would protest.
Andrew Pettigrew had been an unknown quality
and she was gratified by his endorsement. And the
Tremaynes? She'd counted on their support and
was grateful for Abigail's. But Harve? Well, he
hadn't technically opposed her, but neither had he
given her his approval.

What surprised her—okay, scared her—was *her*
reaction to *him*. When he'd looked into her eyes,
she'd felt transparent, as if he could see every one
of her fears and insecurities.

That was bad enough, but her sudden breathless-
ness and the acceleration of her pulse had caught
her completely by surprise. For a moment she'd
been swept back into the past—to those painful
days when Harve Tremayne had been her heart's
desire.

*Not good, Lottie, not good at all,* she chastized
herself. She could excuse her youthful attraction to

him as a typical teenage crush, a case of hero worship, but she was no longer a teenager.

Neither was Harve Tremayne.

He'd developed and honed the leadership abilities he'd exhibited even as a high-school student. Only a few years after taking over management of the family business, he'd guided it into its current position as a Fortune 500 company. At the same time he'd rebuilt the family farm, turning it into a model quarter-horse operation.

Harve was used to taking charge, but business and banking were two different fields of expertise. She didn't need him looking over her shoulder, questioning her every move—which, if she gave him the opportunity, she was sure he'd try to do. And if she couldn't control her physical and emotional response to him, she'd lose her focus.

Acknowledging a twinge of disappointment, she sighed, then swung the car into the overgrown driveway of her childhood home. She mentally began listing tasks to be completed in the next few days. First, arrange for the house to be cleaned. Second, order her household belongings shipped from Saint Louis. Third, purchase what she needed to camp out in the house until she could get settled.

Her old home, known locally as the Blackburn place, had been standing since shortly after Simon Blackburn arrived in Little Falls in the mid-1850s and joined forces with Gideon Tremayne and Ambrose Pettigrew to found the community bank. As a child she hadn't appreciated the antiquity of the house. It had simply been home. She'd loved growing up in the gracious old-fashioned Victorian, with its corner cupola, bow windows and wide wraparound porch.

She remembered the leisurely summer days best, tea parties on the wide porch, chasing fireflies across the lawn in the twilight and searching for katydid "shells" on the trunks of the huge oak trees that shaded the house from the summer heat.

Now, with an adult's appreciation of history and her personal memories, she could hardly wait to move back into the old place. Maybe then she'd feel as if she'd really come home.

Still lost in the happier memories of her past, she parked the car in the carriage entry. It took a moment for reality to penetrate.

Paint hung in strips or had vanished completely from the exterior of the house. Parts of the porch banisters had disappeared, and many of the lacy carved corner braces were missing or hanging askew. Mole tunnels crossed the once-smooth lawn. Weeds choked flower beds and walkways. Leafless dead limbs disfigured the green canopies of the spreading oaks.

She'd believed confronting her uncle was the hardest thing she would ever do. Now she wasn't sure. As she surveyed the decay of her childhood home, she fought a sense of defeat and despair almost as bitter as what she'd felt thirteen years ago.

Had she done the right thing coming back to Little Falls? Would she be able to build a life here, or would the town burden the daughter with the sins of the father?

*Stop it!* she commanded herself. She'd come back to Little Falls for a purpose. She wouldn't, couldn't, let this defeat her. She'd known it wouldn't be easy.

Lottie walked slowly around one side of the house. She could see no broken windows, no signs of vandalism, no graffiti. Not that she'd expected any. After all, Little Falls was not Saint Louis. Time and nature had done this damage.

On the east side of the house she hesitated, reluctant to take that last step around the overgrown boxwood hedge that protected the rose garden. Originally planted by the wife of the first Simon Blackburn, it had been expanded more each generation. Caring for the roses was one thing she'd missed most when her mother had whisked her off to Saint Louis after her father's death.

How many varieties, especially those planted by the first and second Mrs. Blackburns, had been lost through neglect? Some of them, she knew, would no longer be available commercially. Lottie drew a deep breath and forced herself to move around the hedge.

Shock held her momentarily paralyzed. For although it was surrounded by neglect and decay, the rose garden was in perfect condition. Tears stung her eyelids as she struggled to believe what her eyes were seeing.

There were no weeds here. The herringbone brick walkways were clean and level, the beds raked and tidy. Ramblers clung to white trellises, their old-fashioned pink-and-red blooms bright against lush green leaves. And everywhere, the sight and scent of roses in flower, all perfectly pruned and groomed. Not even dropped petals from the early-spring varieties marred the grounds.

But how? Who?

Just then she heard a gasp. She spun around to see the young girl who'd stepped onto the walkway behind her. She blinked, not sure the image was real, but the girl remained. It was like looking into an old photograph album of her childhood. The child was twelve, maybe thirteen years old. Wisps of hair the deep burnished color of a new penny had escaped her braids and curled around her face. She had freckles across the bridge of her nose, a smudge of dirt on her cheek, mud on the knees of her jeans, and light brown eyes wide with surprise and something that looked like fear.

Lottie moved toward her. "Did you do this? Take care of the rose garden?"

The girl retreated a step. "I...I didn't mean any harm."

"Harm? Of course not. The garden is beautiful. Just as I remember it. Thank you for tending it."

She paused, then said, smiling, "I'm Lottie Carlyle. What's your name?"

The girl retreated another step. "Please, don't tell anyone. My father... I'm not supposed to be here." The girl whirled around and, before Lottie could utter a protest, disappeared through a gap in the hedge.

Lottie started to follow, then hesitated. Chasing after the child when she obviously wanted to leave was no way to repay a favor.

In a town as small as Little Falls, Lottie knew she'd be able to learn the girl's identity. Then she'd make it clear to her that she not only didn't mind the intrusion, she appreciated it. The beauty of the garden was a gift, especially welcome amid the sorry state of the house and the rest of the grounds.

Lottie made her way back to the front yard, knowing she couldn't summon the strength to inspect the interior of the house today. It was obvious she wasn't going to be able to live here, not without repairs first.

When a green pickup truck turned into the rutted driveway, she shivered, suddenly aware of her vulnerability. With the house set behind a high overgrown hedge, invisible from the road, she was, to all intents and purposes, isolated here, and she certainly wasn't expecting visitors.

With a rush of relief she recognized Harve Tremayne climbing from the truck's cab. Her relief was short-lived, however, replaced by the same disturbing feelings she'd had earlier when she'd met his gaze across the boardroom table.

He walked toward her, his tall lean body moving in the perfectly coordinated way of a natural athlete.

"Good morning, Lottie," he said, pushing his tan Stetson back from his forehead. "You didn't give me a chance to say welcome home."

She forced breath from her lungs to her vocal cords. "Harve, what are you doing here? Is the board meeting over? How did you find me?"

His lips twitched and his quiet chuckle sent goose bumps dancing down her spine. It wasn't a particularly comfortable feeling.

"Which question should I answer first?" he asked, amusement in his blue eyes. Yes, this was the Harve she remembered—only more potent, more powerful and, she realized, potentially more dangerous to her peace of mind.

"I'm here because I wanted to talk to you," he said. "The house was a logical place to look. As for the board meeting, it wasn't over when I left, but I suspect it soon will be. After your dramatic appearance, anything else will be anticlimactic. A well-planned and well-executed coup." He softened his words with a smile. "Congratulations."

"Thank you, I think," she said. "Surprise seemed the best plan. But if the board meeting's not over, what are you doing here?"

"Suppose I said I wanted to see if the poised

confident woman who executed the coup was really the ragtag scrawny brat who used to torment me?''

He was talking about her *early* childhood, when she and his younger cousin, Vicki Winslow, had followed him around like pesky puppies. Was it possible he didn't remember the summer when she was an adolescent and had made such a fool of herself over him? Or was he ignoring it to spare her feelings?

"That was a long time ago," she said uncomfortably, "but even then, I knew what I wanted." Realizing what she'd said, she felt her cheeks redden.

"No, you were never bashful about voicing your opinions or going after what you wanted," he agreed.

"Well, you should talk, Harvey Tremayne," she protested. "I remember how you used to boss Vicki and me around." She made a sound of disgust. "And we let you."

"Not always." His tone was gently teasing. "I remember when you talked Vicki and me into going swimming in Farmer Miller's stock pond—wearing only our underwear."

As Lottie remembered that particular adventure, she again felt herself blush. Darn it, she didn't want him to know how he was affecting her. "Vicki and I were only about seven," she said, feigning offense. "You were a much older man—at least eleven. Besides, I didn't talk you into anything. I simply said I was going. You and Vicki decided to come, too. I also remember being thoroughly walloped when we were caught."

The expression on his face was somber, but his eyes still glinted with humor. "I was barely ten," he corrected, "and you and Vicki escaped with a couple of light swats on the rear. I, on the other hand, couldn't sit down for a week."

Lottie failed to suppress a grin, but managed to keep a mock haughty tone in her voice. "As the oldest and most responsible, you were, of course, the more culpable. It was only fair that you received the more severe punishment."

"My grandmother said something similar," Harve admitted. "You know, until today, I hadn't thought of that summer in years. Now I remember praying daily for September to arrive and Vicki to go home. The two of you could get into more mischief than kittens in a milking shed."

His mouth twisted in a grin. "I guess Thomas Fuller was right," he added. "'That which is bitter to endure may be sweet to remember.'"

"Only some things," she said, hating, but unable to prevent, the huskiness in her voice. "Others are as bitter as ever."

For a long moment a silence stretched taut between them. "Well," Harve finally drawled, as if searching for something to restore the previous mood, "I've learned one thing, anyway. You still rise to the bait—magnificently."

"And you can still talk the ears off a mule," she rallied. "Why did you follow me out here, Harve?"

"I need to know why you came back," he said bluntly.

"Why? Because Little Falls is my home and the bank my inheritance, just as it's yours. Now if that's all you wanted, you're going to have to excuse me. I have a lot to do before reporting to work Monday."

He shook his head. "If the board meeting was any indication, the field is yours."

"That's wishful thinking," she told him. "Uncle Cyrus may be forced to accept my presence, but that doesn't mean he'll step meekly aside. He's had power too long. I'm going to have two fights on my hands and you know it—one with Uncle Cyrus for control and the other to save the bank. As a member of the board of directors, how could you allow the bank to get in such trouble? Didn't you see what was happening? Didn't you *care?*"

The expression that flickered across his face was impossible to read. "Yes, I saw, and yes, I cared, but there wasn't a hell of a lot I could do about it," he told her, his voice almost a growl. "Even with the backing of Grandmother and Andrew Pettigrew, I could only muster forty percent support. Cyrus controlled the rest. Besides, I couldn't have taken over. I'm no banker."

"Well, I am," she said flatly, "but if you felt that way, why didn't you support me in there?" She realized her voice carried a hint of accusation and disappointment.

He took a deep breath. "Look, Lottie, I didn't *not* support you. I completely agree that something has to be done, but I don't like buying a pig in a poke. I need to know what you're planning."

She wasn't surprised. He'd made it clear he wasn't going to give her his support carte blanche. "I don't know what I'm going to do until I get into the bank records and can assess exactly what kind of position we're in," she replied. "Believe me, when I select a course of action, you and the rest of the board will be the first to know. Now, as I said earlier, you'll have to excuse me. I really do have things to do."

Harve rocked back on his heels. "Like what? I'm not simply being nosy, you know. There's a chance I can help."

She hesitated, debating with herself. Was his offer sincere? Asking him for assistance might put her in his debt, but did she have any choice? "If you really want to help...do you happen to know of a place in town suitable to rent?"

It took him a moment to react. "You intended to stay here, didn't you? Surely you realized what kind of shape the house would be in after sitting empty all these years."

Lottie shrugged, pretending it didn't matter. "I thought my mother had arranged for at least minimal maintenance—which just proves I'm still the eternal optimist. I should've realized she essentially abandoned the house when she left Little Falls.''

"I'm sorry, Lottie. It must be hard seeing it like this. Have you been inside?''

She shook her head, afraid to trust her voice.

"It might not be so bad,'' he said gently. The regret in his voice seemed sincere. "Would you like me to come with you? We can make a quick survey.''

"No,'' she said when she managed to speak. "It doesn't matter how bad it is, I'll fix it, but obviously not by Monday. Meanwhile I need a place to rent. Any ideas?''

Harve frowned. "No, I don't. Look, why don't you come out to the farm with me? I suspect Grandmother will be along as soon as the board meeting breaks up. If anyone knows of a possible rental, she will.''

"I don't want to impose—''

"Hey, when people are caught together au naturel, surely they can be considered friends. Friends don't impose.''

He flashed her a smile and she felt her pulse rate double. She cleared her throat, wanting to deny the way he affected her. "I'm not sure—''

"She's your best lead in finding some place to live.'' He shifted his weight from one foot to the other as if impatient to be gone.

She hesitated another moment, but knew he was right. Abigail Tremayne *was* her best source for suggestions. So much for her earlier resolve to avoid Harve. "Okay, I'll come."

"Fine," he said, "and in case you've forgotten the way, you can follow me." Then without giving her chance to change her mind, he turned and walked to his truck.

Drawing a deep breath, Lottie hurried after him. She could only pray she wasn't making a mistake.

## CHAPTER THREE

LOTTIE HAD TO GRIN as she followed Harve through the back door into the farmhouse kitchen. No dead bolts, door chains or peepholes here. She'd bet the front doors of most homes in Little Falls hadn't been opened since welcoming carolers at Christmastime, not unless an out-of-town Bible salesman had happened by. In Little Falls both friends and family always used the back door.

It was this simple more casual lifestyle she craved—green pasture landscapes instead of grime-coated buildings, breezes wafting the scent of fresh-cut hay instead of exhaust fumes, trust in the good of your fellow man instead of suspicion and fear.

She glanced at her host and found him studying her with a curious intensity.

"Private joke?" he asked, a note of cynicism in his voice.

She refused to let him destroy her mood. "Not at all. I was just remembering…happy times." She thought she saw his eyes soften before he looked away.

"I'll get you a cup of coffee while we wait for

Grandmother,'' he told her, reaching into a cupboard. ''I need to check the foaling barn for a minute, but my housekeeper, Annie Martin, is around somewhere. She'll keep you company.''

Lottie was momentarily stunned. ''Annie Martin's your housekeeper?'' she finally managed to ask, her voice choked with emotion.

''Oh, that's right. I forgot. Annie used to work for your family, didn't she?'' He turned his blue-eyed gaze on her, his expression friendly.

Lottie nodded. ''Yes, she did. I can't wait to see her again.''

''I suspect she'll be glad to see you too. Coffee's on the stove.'' He handed her an empty mug. ''Sugar and cream's on the counter. Help yourself and I'll go find her.''

Lottie clutched the mug tightly, her memories of Annie Martin almost overwhelming her. Even in better days, before her father's death and the move to Saint Louis, Sarah Carlyle had never played the role of mother well. She'd preferred to delegate those duties. Generous jovial Annie Martin, with her loving heart and homespun philosophy had been everything Sarah Carlyle hadn't been during Lottie's growing-up years.

After the move to Saint Louis, Lottie had mourned the loss of Annie almost as much as the loss of her father, especially when Sarah's embittered retreat from life essentially left her without a mother.

When she heard the sound of rapidly approaching footsteps, Lottie set the still-empty cup on the table and turned toward the swinging door that separated the kitchen from the rest of the house. She had only a second to notice that Annie was a little older and a little rounder than she remembered before she was enfolded in a warm hug.

"God love it, is it really you, Miss Lottie? Let me look at you."

Even though she was now half a head taller than the elderly housekeeper, Lottie felt about ten years old as Annie inspected her from head to toe.

"All grown-up and so pretty, too." Annie dabbed at her eyes with the hem of her apron, and Lottie felt moisture swim in her own.

"Oh, Annie, it's so good to see you."

"I could hardly believe it when Mr. Harve told me you were here," Annie said, shaking her head. "I must say, it's past time you came home. Why'd you stay away so long? Oh, never mind. It doesn't matter now. The important thing is you're here. Set yourself down. I've got fresh cinnamon buns. Baked this morning."

Lottie laughed. "Still trying to fatten me up, Annie?"

"Somebody better. Looks like a good wind would blow you away."

"I think you look just fine," Harve drawled from the doorway, "but have one, anyway. Annie's cinnamon buns are ambrosia."

Lottie turned at the sound of his voice. He'd taken time to change into work clothes, and her first thought was that the way the man filled out a chambray shirt ought to be declared illegal. There was a tingling in her midsection as she battled the unwelcome surge of attraction. "I remember," she said softly.

It was Harve who broke eye contact first, his attention returning to his housekeeper. "I expect my grandmother will be along in a few minutes, Annie. Call me when she arrives, would you? I'll be in the foaling barn. I need to check on Pretty Lady."

"Oh, my," Annie said. "In all the excitement, I forgot to tell you. Dr. Peterson called from the barn right before you got here. Pretty Lady's fine. Her little filly, too. Said if he was gone before you got back, he'd check in later."

Harve gave a genuine smile of pleasure. "A filly? I should've known. It's always the females who cause trouble." The mock-complaint of his words contradicted the expression of satisfaction on his face, but Lottie couldn't help wondering if his words were the more accurate barometer of his feelings—particularly where she was concerned.

"Get along with you, Mr. Harve," Annie told him. "I know you were hoping for a filly. Go on now. Miss Lottie and I'll be just fine. We've got some catching up to do."

Abigail Tremayne arrived at the farm only

minutes after Harve disappeared in the direction of the barn.

"Call me Abby, dear," she told Lottie. "We may not be exactly contemporaries, but we are both adults. So, are you going to be able to save the bank?"

Abigail Tremayne had never been one, Lottie remembered, to beat around the bush. "I'm going to try." She met the older woman's penetrating gaze, struggling not to show her nervousness.

"Forgive me," Abby said, "but I had to be sure. The opportunity for revenge against your uncle must surely be tempting."

Lottie shook her head. "I have no particular love for my uncle," she admitted, "but the animosity between him and my mother was as much her doing as his." She hesitated deliberately before continuing, deciding to be completely forthright. "My mother believed that Uncle Cyrus was the embezzler, not my father," she said carefully, "but I can't accuse him without evidence and I can't blame him for believing what everyone else in town believes—that my father was guilty."

"Your father—"

"He *was* probably guilty," Lottie interrupted, "but even if he wasn't and someone could prove it, it wouldn't affect the bank's situation today. I'm my father's daughter, but I'm also a Blackburn. My ancestors helped found the bank. I don't want to see it fail."

"Neither do I, my dear," Abby said after a moment, "but the present predicament is not your fault. Cyrus, the pompous old troglodyte, can claim that honor."

Lottie couldn't help smiling at Abby's description of her uncle. Cyrus was some thirty years younger, but only chronologically. Abigail Tremayne's spirit would never grow old. Lottie wondered if her uncle's had *ever* been young.

"I must say, you certainly managed to surprise everyone this morning," Abby said. "Showing up at the board meeting like that is going to have tongues wagging all over town."

"My lawyer suggested I not give Uncle Cyrus any warning."

"It worked. Caught him flat-footed." Abigail laughed. "Never thought I'd see Cyrus Blackburn reduced to stuttering."

"Now that's a sight I'd like to have seen," Annie said. "Bet it was a better show than the time Louisa Barkley and Mazie Parsons showed up at church in the same hat."

"That it was, Annie," Abby agreed.

When Abby asked her if there was anything she could do to help her get settled, Lottie didn't hesitate.

"I'd intended to stay at the old house in town, but I hadn't realized it was in such bad shape," Lottie told her. "Harve thought you might know of a place I could rent for a while."

"No need to worry about that," Abby said, dismissing the problem with a wave of her hand. "You'll stay with me of course."

The offer was completely unexpected, and Lottie struggled to find the right words to refuse without appearing ungracious. "Oh, no. I mean, I couldn't impose on you, although I appreciate the offer."

"Only other place in town would be Louisa Barkley's boardinghouse," Annie said, "and she's the worst busybody in Little Falls. We don't have much call for rentals around here."

"There's no imposition involved, dear," Abby said with an imperial shake of her head. "I rattle around in the old place like a dried pea. Besides, there's a self-contained apartment at the back of the house. Had it built for a live-in physical therapist a couple of years ago when I fell and broke my hip. It has its own entrance so you can have all the privacy you want. And when you feel like visiting, well, I'll enjoy the company."

Abby's place, a gracious old home that had been in her family since before she'd married a Tremayne, was just down the road from Harve's farm. Lottie realized the offer was probably the best solution to her problem. Still, she was reluctant. Would she be able to avoid Harve, his interference, if she was living almost next door? If she was living with his grandmother?

"I still don't think—"

"You might as well give in gracefully, Lottie. No one wins arguments with my grandmother."

*Think of the devil...* Lottie whirled around to find Harve leaning against the kitchen door frame. His expression gave no hint of his thoughts. Hers, on the other hand, were probably as easy to read as a first-grade primer.

"How long have you been there?"

"Only long enough to hear you trying to say no to my grandmother, and I tell you now, it's wasted effort."

"Fiddle-faddle," Abby snorted. "Charlotte will agree because it's the best solution." She turned back to Lottie. "In addition to giving you a place to stay, it won't do any harm to let folks know you have my support. That'll be plain enough if you're staying with me."

"Grandmother's right, you know," Harve said. "Such an obvious vote of confidence from her will influence how quickly and easily you're accepted back into the community."

He was speaking about his grandmother's support, but was careful not to commit his own, Lottie noted.

"It'll weaken the gossip about your dad, too," Annie added cheerfully, "and likely dilute some of Cyrus's complaining. I'll stop and have a cup of tea with Myrtle at the Down Home on my way through town this afternoon. The news'll be all over Little Falls by morning."

Lottie frowned. "I don't see how."

"It hasn't been *that* long since you lived here." Harve chuckled. "There's not a lot to do but talk about the other residents—and former residents. Prodigal sons and daughters make the best stories of all. But don't worry. Wasn't it George Eliot who said, 'As to people saying a few idle words about us, we must not mind that any more than the old church steeple minds the rooks cawing about it'?"

That was the second time he'd spouted a quotation at her, Lottie realized. She'd forgotten how he sprinkled his speech with obscure words from long-dead writers, recruiting their opinions to endorse his own. The habit had irritated her as a teenager. It still did.

"You'll soon learn our ways again," Annie assured her. "As long as you remember there's not much goes on around here somebody else don't know, you'll do fine."

Annie was right. Abby's seal of approval would dilute some of the gossip about her father that her return was certain to resurrect. She hadn't anticipated such an obvious public endorsement.

There were disadvantages, too—mainly Abby's handsome six-foot-three grandson. She would have preferred to maintain a certain distance. Harve had made it plain he wasn't giving her his complete support until he knew her plans. She might have another battle there, and the idea of Harve Tremayne as an opponent made Uncle Cyrus seem like a marshmallow. Living in his grandmother's home, she'd be unable to avoid him. But did she have a choice?

She looked helplessly from Annie to Harve, then to his grandmother, and finally gave in. "Thank you for your invitation," she said, hoping her voice carried no hint of her reluctance. "I'll try not to be a bother."

Abby and Annie beamed their approval. Harve's expression was inscrutable.

LOTTIE FOUND HERSELF comfortably settled into the apartment at the back of Abby's house by nightfall. Pleading fatigue, she was able to thwart Abby's suggestion that Harve "take her out for a celebration dinner." It wasn't a lie. She *was* tired, so tired she barely found the energy for a warm shower before falling into bed. Her exhaustion, she suspected, was as much mental as physical.

She spent the remaining days of the week doing a variety of tasks, including making arrangements to store her household possessions in nearby Fayetteville and negotiating with a contractor, recommended by Harve, for renovation work at her house.

On one such visit to the house, she showed Harve the rose garden and described the girl she'd seen there. "Do you have any idea who she is?" Lottie asked.

He shrugged. "Does it matter? I'm sure you'll find her. Little Falls isn't that big."

Something in his expression told her he knew more than he was telling. "You *do* know who she is," Lottie accused.

"I can guess," he admitted, "but I may be wrong. Besides, if she's who I think she is, you'll find out soon enough."

*Stubborn man,* Lottie thought when he refused to say anything else, in spite of her attempts to get him to change his mind.

Sunday, Harve accompanied Lottie and his grandmother to the local community church—an excursion that left Lottie's head spinning as she tried to sort out names and faces.

"Don't worry about it," Abby advised. "Most of us have known each other since the day we were born. You'll be able to match names and faces in no time."

Lottie suspected that some of the residents who'd greeted her were more curious than welcoming, but at least she didn't meet overt hostility. Apparently the shield of Abby Tremayne's sponsorship was working. No one would have dared be rude to the elderly woman or her guest.

And if Lottie'd had any doubts about Harve's position of influence in the community, they were quickly dispelled when Isaac Easton, owner of the Little Falls general store, approached them.

He greeted Lottie and Abby courteously, then

turned his attention to Harve. "Have you heard anything new about that developer's plans to build a shopping center out on the highway?" Isaac asked.

"As a matter of fact, I hear the plans are on hold," Harve told him.

"But for how long?"

"For a few years, anyway," Harve said. "I understand the land's no longer available."

Lottie saw the look of relief on Isaac's face. "The Downtown Merchants Association will be glad to hear that," he said.

"The Downtown Merchants need to finish that application for historical designation and use the grant money for restoration work along Main Street," Harve told him. "Once that's completed, development along the highway will draw more people downtown, rather than threatening the downtown with bankruptcy."

Although his tone was conversational, Lottie couldn't help noticing that Isaac reacted as if Harve had given him an order.

"I'll call a meeting this week," the store owner said. "We'll get it ready before the end of the month."

Harve handed Isaac a card. "If the association has any questions, you can contact my attorney. He's successfully shepherded a couple of similar applications through the red tape."

"Sounds like it might be a good idea for him to

look it over before we submit it," Isaac said, although there was a questioning look on his face.

"It wouldn't hurt," Harve said. "I'll tell him to expect your call. Consider his bill my contribution to the cause."

"And what other contributions did you make?" Lottie heard Abby ask softly as Isaac walked away. "How much did the land cost you?"

Harve shrugged. "I'll make a profit in a few years, and in the meantime the land's off the market. No land, no shopping mall." He turned to Lottie. "You didn't hear that," he said.

"Hear what?" she said. "But what happens with the next project? You can't stop progress, Harve. Not all by yourself."

"Of course not," he replied. "All I've done is buy the downtown area some time. It's up to them to use it wisely. Hopefully, when the next development is proposed, the merchants will be able take advantage of additional business activity in the area, instead of being threatened by it."

Lottie couldn't help being impressed. The Tremaynes had been movers and shakers in Little Falls since the town's inception. Harve had more or less inherited his leadership position in the community. He was also wealthy enough to make things happen his way. Either circumstance could easily cause the town's residents to resent him—and she supposed they would if he bullied them into accepting his opinions.

Instead, he'd learned, it seemed, to temper the take-charge gung ho attitude of his youth and adopt a subtler approach, gently nudging others in the direction he thought best. He wasn't above using his wealth to interfere when necessary, and apparently anonymously, then suggesting alternative solutions and allowing others to instigate them.

Lottie was more convinced than ever that, if she was going to save the bank, she would need Harve's cooperation and approval; but she also knew she needed to set the agenda.

MONDAY MORNING Lottie purposely timed her arrival at the bank for a few minutes after nine, knowing most of the staff would already be at work.

Cyrus unlocked the front doors to let her enter—the bank didn't open until ten for customers. "We begin our working day promptly at nine," he said by way of greeting, not bothering to disguise his displeasure.

Lottie refused to play his game. "Good morning, Uncle Cyrus." She gave him a smile. "I like to get an early start, too. Thank you for letting me in. I'll have a set of keys made today so I won't have to disturb you in the future."

For a moment she thought he was going to protest, but evidently he thought better of the idea. "Have Jefferson make copies for you," he said gruffly, then retreated to his office and closed the door, leaving her standing in the middle of the lobby.

"Old goat," Lottie muttered under her breath. Cyrus wasn't going to make it easy, but then, she really hadn't expected him to. The best she could hope for was that sometime in the future they'd find a tolerable coexistence.

Last week she'd been so focused on her confrontation with the board she'd paid little attention to the area where customers were serviced. Now, glancing around, she noticed that the carpeting was clean and in good condition. Above the dark mahogany wainscoting, the walls appeared freshly painted. Several of the polished brass spittoons she remembered from her childhood were still in evidence, though all but one now served as planters for low-maintenance greenery. The solitary holdout was positioned just inside the marble slab entry and was half filled with white sand.

Good, she thought. Nothing shabby. The furnishings reflected tradition and stability, giving no hint of financial difficulties, although she didn't doubt that at least part of the situation was public knowledge.

She felt a sense of being watched and turned in time to see a woman in the teller's cage quickly avert her eyes. She was attractive and appeared to be in her early thirties. Lottie didn't recognize her.

Lottie hesitated for a moment, then walked over to the cage. "Good morning," she said, "I'm Lottie Carlyle. As I'm sure you've heard, I'm going to be working here.''

The woman's mouth twitched. Maybe it was supposed to be a smile, but it disappeared so quickly Lottie couldn't be sure.

"I'm Josephine Winters."

When it became apparent the woman wasn't going to say anything more, Lottie tried again. "Winters? I remember a Winters family. They used to live out on the Lake Highway."

"They still do. Leon's my husband."

"I knew Leon," Lottie told her. "He's a couple of years older than me. His sister, Patricia, and I were in the same class."

"Leon runs the farm now. Pat lives in Little Rock."

Obviously Josephine Winters wasn't given to idle conversation, Lottie thought, watching as the woman finished loading two cash tills. Josephine slipped one till into the teller drawer in front of her, then placed the other in the drawer at the next station, locked it and dropped the key into her own drawer.

"Well, when you talk to Pat, tell her I said hello."

"All right," Josephine said without looking up. She opened another drawer and began arranging pens, rubber stamps and other supplies in her workstation.

"Who works the second cage?" Lottie asked,

hoping this time she'd draw a few more words from the woman.

"Nobody, unless we get really busy. Then, if Jeff, I mean, Mr. Blackburn, is available, he'll help."

"But you prepare the drawer every day?"

"Just on Mondays. It's our busiest day."

"I would have thought Fridays were busier. That's the usual payday."

Josephine shrugged. "The bank closes at three-thirty, so the wives bring in their husbands' paychecks on Mondays."

So much for that, Lottie thought. Either Josephine Winters wasn't inclined to become friendly quickly or she'd been instructed to offer no help to the new kid on the block.

"Well, if you get busy today, call me," Lottie said. "It's going to take me a while to learn the bank's routine, but I can handle a teller's cage. It'll be a good way to start meeting the bank's customers."

This time Josephine didn't answer, but after a moment's hesitation, she nodded her head.

Lottie took another quick glance around the empty lobby, then walked toward the door that had been her father's office. The door to the next office was standing open, and she could see Jefferson behind his desk, apparently concentrating on the computer screen in front of him. She'd been going to ignore him, then decided to say hello. Cyrus, Jefferson and everyone else in the bank could try to pretend she wasn't here, but she at least was not going to be accused of being rude.

"Good morning, Jefferson."

Her cousin looked up, surprise on his face, but he recovered quickly. "Good morning, Charlotte. I'm sorry, I didn't know you'd arrived. When did you get here?"

"Only a few minutes ago. I waited until I was sure someone would be here to let me in. Cyrus said you'd have a set of keys made for me today."

He nodded. "Sure. I guess you'd like to see your office and get settled in." He took a key from the top drawer, then stood and walked around his desk to offer it to her. "This one fits your office door. I'll have copies of the front- and back-door keys made for you later today."

He stood a little behind her as she turned the lock and pushed open the door.

Lottie's gaze quickly swept the room. A walnut pedestal desk stood in front of the window, and nearby was a computer on a rolling stand. Two file cabinets were positioned against the wall. There was also a comfortable-looking desk chair and two occasional chairs, all upholstered in dark green leather. The desktop had been polished to a high gloss, and a crystal bud vase containing a single yellow rose had been set in one corner.

Lottie's voice caught in her throat. She'd almost been expecting a desk made of a board resting on a pair of orange crates, especially after the chilly welcome she'd had from her uncle Cyrus and Josephine Winters. "I didn't think...I mean, it's very nice. Did you do this, Jefferson?"

"Only the heavy work—moving the furniture and such. Jeannie got me organized and did most of the cleaning. She said you'd want to add your own personal touches, like pictures and things. She sent the rose. As a welcome."

"Jeannie?"

"My wife." This was said with pride.

"Oh, Jefferson, I should've known. I'm sorry."

"No reason for you to be. She wants to meet you, though. Said she'd be happy to know anyone who stood up to my father."

Lottie swallowed a chuckle. "I want to meet her, too. I like her already."

Jefferson gave Lottie a quick smile before his expression turned solemn. "Look, Charlotte, I'm sorry about the way I acted at the board meeting. Jeannie says I don't react well to surprises. If we're going to be working together, I'd like us to be friends."

Lottie studied him a minute. Why was he suddenly being so nice? Did he really mean it or was he up to something? One thing for sure, considering the hostility she'd encountered so far, she couldn't afford to turn down any gestures of cooperation. She decided to accept his offer, but she'd stay on guard.

She held out her hand. "I'd like to be friends, too." She paused. "Do you think you could call me Lottie?"

An expression of something like relief crossed his features as he took her hand. "Done, if you'll call me Jeff. Only my father calls me Jefferson." Then he grinned. "And Jeannie—when she's mad at me."

In the thirty minutes that remained before the bank's doors opened for business, her cousin escorted her around the premises, introducing her to the other bank employees. The bookkeeper, Hiram Nelson, was a mousy little man with a bald pate and thick horn-rimmed glasses. He took only enough time to glance up from his desk and nod in her direction. Cyrus's secretary, the elderly Emma Whitehall, was barely civil—not much of a change from the days when Lottie had stopped by after school to visit her father.

Jeff showed her where supplies were stored and furnished her with a copy of the computer's general-access codes, then, when a customer requested to see him, left her on her own. As soon as he disappeared, Emma marched into her office without bothering to knock.

She might have been an attractive woman if the expression on her face wasn't so sour, Lottie thought. Emma's once dark hair was now mostly gray, her back was ramrod straight, and she wore her plain dark skirt and white starched blouse like a uniform.

"Can I help you, Emma?" Lottie asked, determined to be pleasant.

"I simply wanted to inform you that my time is fully occupied with my work for Cyrus...Mr. Blackburn," Emma said. "I do not have time to add secretarial duties for you to my workload."

"I understand," Lottie said. And certainly this was no loss, she thought. Cyrus and Emma made a good pair—both rigid unpleasant individuals. If public relations depended on those two, it was a miracle the bank had survived this long.

Lottie had done her own filing before, and she could do it again. It was probably better, anyway. She didn't particularly want Cyrus to know what she was doing until she was ready to tell him— something that would be impossible to achieve if Emma had access to her files.

The rest of the day passed in a blur. Apparently Annie's prediction that her return to town would be the hot topic of the day was correct. She was surprised at the number of bank customers who requested to see her, although she suspected it was more curiosity than welcome.

Josephine didn't call for her, but several times during the day, when the line in the lobby grew particularly long, she went to the second teller's cage and was silently handed the key to the drawer.

Although she was used to working a much longer

day, by the time the bank's doors closed at three, Lottie was exhausted.

It was the newness and the tension, she told herself. Things would get better. She tallied the teller's drawer, signed and dated the tape and handed it to Josephine, then returned to her office.

Lottie sank into her chair with a sigh. One day and already her desk was a disaster zone, papers and files stacked haphazardly.

Josephine's comments this morning about banking hours had given her a couple of ideas. She'd do a demographic study of the bank's current customers first, but if what she suspected was true, later banking hours on Fridays or maybe several hours Saturday morning would be a draw for new customers. The bank's revenues were down, and the quickest way to fix that was to increase the volume of business. Once a broader customer base was established, she could take a closer look at the bank's other operations.

Lottie began sorting papers and folders, sliding them into the desktop filing trays she'd requisitioned from the storeroom this morning. She picked up a plain white envelope and paused, turning it in her hand. It was sealed, with nothing to indicate what it was, who it was for or who had sent it.

She frowned, then reached for her letter opener, reasoning that, if it wasn't meant for her, she'd forward it to where it needed to go. She slipped the

single sheet of paper from the envelope and unfolded it.

The message was short, simple and easy to
read—large letters cut from a variety of newspaper
and magazine headlines and pasted onto the paper
to form three sentences:

WHy Did YOU CoME BACK? NO one
WANTs YOU herE! LEAVE or YOU'll be
SORRY.

## CHAPTER FOUR

LOTTIE INHALED SHARPLY as fear shot through her.

Who was threatening her?

Whoever it was, he'd been anxious to deliver his message. Someone wanted her gone. Now.

She knew that there were Little Falls residents who didn't want her here, knew that her return had prompted belated shame over the way she and her mother were shunned after her father's death. But who felt guilty enough or threatened enough by her presence to resort to an anonymous warning?

A dozen bank customers had paraded through her office today, all prominent community residents, all former friends and associates of her parents. Many visits, however, didn't involve banking business. They were courtesy calls—to welcome her back and wish her well.

But Lottie had read the questions in their eyes.

How much did she remember? Would she try to avenge old slights? The next time Isaac Easton's general store needed an advance to cover a stock order, would she say no? And Myron and Wanda Lawson? Would she approve a loan when they needed funds to meet expenses until harvest?

Would she support Mildred Gaston as chairman of the town's historical society, or would she demand her resignation, as Mildred had once demanded Sarah Carlyle's?

Any one of them or a half-dozen others with similar concerns could have snuck the threatening note onto her desk.

Lottie held the piece of paper to the light, looking for a watermark, for any clue as to the sender. But the paper was as generic as a glass of tap water and the precisely cut and pasted words seemed to mock her.

A neat freak?

Could it be Cyrus?

She supposed it was possible, but her uncle had told her bluntly he didn't want her here. For some reason, she couldn't imagine him clipping messages from magazines to anonymously make a statement he'd essentially already delivered.

What about Jeff? True, he'd seemed welcoming today, but she remembered his hostility at the board meeting. As owner of fifteen percent of the shares and heir to his father's fifteen percent, he had the most to lose by her return. Someday, assuming the bank survived, he and she would own equal shares.

If she'd remained an absentee stockholder, Jefferson would have been the obvious choice to take over the bank after Cyrus's retirement. Her return had set up a future power struggle. Eventually she and her cousin would go head-to-head for control.

Did Jeff feel threatened? Threatened enough to try driving her out of town with an anonymous note?

Lottie carefully laid the paper facedown on her desk and leaned her head against the back of her chair as she tried to sort through other possibilities. As for the other board members, both Abigail Tremayne and Andrew Pettigrew had welcomed her return. Harve remained uncommitted, but she couldn't imagine him hiding behind an unsigned threat.

What about the other bank employees—Josephine Winters, Emma Whitehall or Hiram Nelson? Did they feel threatened by the changing of the guard? Wouldn't common sense suggest they wait, at least long enough to see if they could adjust to the new order? Besides, they had to know that, without drastic changes, the bank would close, eliminating their jobs, anyway.

Lottie sighed. There were simply too many suspects.

So what should she do? Take it to the police?

She knew her return had resurrected the gossip about her father's theft and suicide. The news she was being threatened would be an added juicy tidbit and probably all over town within hours. She saw no reason to provide the old stories with new fuel, especially when the chance of discovering the culprit's identity was practically nonexistent.

There was another consideration, too. Any suggestion of division within the bank, particularly something as intriguing as threats against her, would weaken the bank's already shaky reputation. Even Cyrus recognized that. As adamantly as he opposed her return, he'd been careful to keep his disapproval confined to the boardroom.

Her only two confidants in town were Abigail and Annie. She didn't want to discuss it with either of her two elderly friends because they would do nothing but worry. No, her only option was to keep her own counsel, at least for now.

Decision made, she picked up the note and carefully tucked it back into the envelope, then shoved it into her briefcase. Suddenly anxious to leave, she logged off her computer, grabbed her purse and started across the lobby.

"Hey, Lottie, wait up a second."

She stopped short, then turned to face Jeff.

"I have your keys," he said, dropping them into her hand. "The larger one fits the front door, the small one, the back entrance. If you come in after-hours, remember you have forty-five seconds to reset the alarm."

"I'll remember," she told him, looking into his face. The expression in his eyes was guileless, friendly.

*So, what did you expect? A sign across his forehead announcing "I did it"?* His smile failed to convince her he was innocent, but, she reminded herself, he was no greater a suspect than several others. She forced an answering smile. "Thanks, Jeff. I'll see you tomorrow."

"I'll be here," he said.

*And so will I,* she promised silently.

IN THE DAYS that followed, Lottie's life settled into more of a routine. The notoriety surrounding William Carlyle's prodigal daughter fell into second place on the gossip top-ten list following the county sheriff's Tuesday-night raid on the poker game in the back room of Charlie Zimmermann's barbershop. The raid also caught city councilmen Tom Farley and Doc Stevens, Little Falls's only medical practitioner, but a fourth man had apparently slipped away only minutes before the sheriff arrived.

Speculation about the raid and especially about the identity of the fourth man at the poker table permeated the town. Although the public-gambling charges were only misdemeanors, it was enough to divert attention from Lottie.

Then Joe Crawley, a rancher on the edge of town, lost his prize bull to a stray bullet, presumed fired by an out-of-season hunter, and Lottie's gossip quotient plummeted even further.

It wasn't that she wished anyone bad luck, but she did admit to being grateful that folks had someone else to talk about. With that in mind, she finally decided to face the one challenge she'd been avoiding—a visit to the Down Home Café.

The town's only restaurant, the Down Home, had served Little Falls as eating place and message center for longer than Lottie could remember. It was also the place to discover and discuss the latest gossip. Perversely, if a person wanted to avoid being the object of gossip, he or she had better make at least an occasional foray into the lion's den.

Late Thursday afternoon, after the high-school crowd had cleared out and before the supper rush began, Lottie entered the Down Home. A small bell hanging over the entrance announced her arrival—exactly as it had during her last visit a lifetime ago. She'd been a high-school senior then, her most serious problem a decision on what to wear to that week's pre-football-game pep rally.

For a moment she stood just inside the door as the memories rolled over her. Everything seemed exactly as she remembered, from the red-and-white-checked oilcloth coverings on the tables to the chalkboard menu hanging behind the old-fashioned cash register.

Café owner Myrtle Goodman was in her usual place behind the counter, her appearance defying her sixty-five-plus years. Myrtle's hair was still blond—dyed, of course—and her truck-stop waitress uniform was still a little too short and a little too tight.

With hair permed and face painted Myrtle had caused a sensation when she'd arrived in Little Falls in 1953 on the arm of her new husband, returning

Korean War hero Chester Goodman. "She's bold and brassy as a ten-man marching band, but she's got a heart as big as the Ozarks and she's all mine," Chester had announced to one and all, including his very proper mother, who'd reportedly taken one look at her new daughter-in-law and retired to her bed with heart palpitations.

Lottie hadn't been born yet, but in typical Little Falls tradition, which refused to let a good story die, she'd heard the tale often enough as a child to be able to imagine being there.

Chester had "gone to his reward" several years ago, and Myrtle had lived up to her late husband's expectations, earning her place in the community and in the hearts of Little Falls residents.

Moving more from remembered habit than conscious thought, Lottie slid onto one of the cushioned stools that lined the counter.

"Well, missy, it's about time you stopped by," declared Myrtle. "I was beginning to think you'd grown too big-city to patronize this little old place."

"You know better than that, Mrs. Goodman," she said, shaking her head and smiling. "I've just been busy trying to settle in."

"Hmph," Myrtle snorted. "More than likely you were waiting for some of the gossip to die down." Her voice was more matter-of-fact than accusing. "Not that I blame you," she added, her expression gentling into a welcoming smile. "If I had a dollar for every time I've heard your name the last couple of weeks, I could close up this place and retire. There's been more talk about you showing up out of the blue than there was the time Preacher Riley ran off with Deacon Harlow's wife.''

It wasn't exactly the news Lottie had hoped for, but she wasn't surprised, either. She sighed. "I was afraid of that.''

"Well, if it's any comfort, the talk's started to quiet down some lately,'' Myrtle confided.

Lottie grinned. "I guess I can thank the county sheriff for that. And Mr. Zimmermann.''

Myrtle wiped at the already clean counter with a towel. "If you're passing out thank-yous, you might as well add Billy Bob, the police chief, to that list. Everyone in town knows Zimmermann's been holding his Tuesday-night poker games for years. If Billy Bob hadn't started making noises about maybe running for sheriff, Eldon would never have come up with the idea for the raid. He only wanted to embarrass Billy Bob on his own turf, so to speak.''

Lottie couldn't help but laugh. "I wondered about that. As I recall, Mr. Zimmermann's Tuesday-night games weren't exactly a secret, even when I was a kid.''

Myrtle leaned forward and with a grin Lottie could only describe as conspiratorial said, "Last laugh's on Eldon, though. Word is Billy Bob left the game to investigate a dog howling behind

Louisa Barkley's boardinghouse about ten minutes before Eldon arrived. Wouldn't that've been a hoot? The county sheriff arresting Little Falls's police chief for illegal gambling. Incidentally we've got a contribution jar set up by the cash register to help Zimmermann, Farley and Doc pay their fines. Doesn't seem fair they should have to pay for Billy Bob's foolishness. He's got no intentions of running for county sheriff. Just wanted to rile Eldon.''

She paused for breath. ''Now, what can I get you? Or did you come in just to visit?''

''Mostly to visit,'' Lottie admitted, ''but I'll have a glass of iced tea. Do you still serve it with lemon and fresh mint?''

''Didn't know there was any other way, but I've got supper up if you'd like to eat. Tonight's menu is Salisbury steak, mashed potatoes and fresh fried okra. With biscuits and gravy, of course.''

Cholesterol heaven or not, it made Lottie's mouth water. ''That sounds delicious,'' she said, ''but I told Mrs. Tremayne I'd join her for supper tonight. I'm staying at her house, you know.''

''Well, 'course, I know. So does everyone else in town,'' Myrtle said. Then, her brow furrowed, she added, ''I don't blame you for laying low for a while, but now's the time to start circulating a bit, honey. You ought to know that nothing causes more talk in this town than trying to avoid it.''

''What have people been say—?'' With a furtive glance toward the back of the room, Lottie broke off. She recognized old Sam Taylor, looking only slightly more ancient than he had a decade ago, sitting at a back table playing checkers with another grizzled old-timer she didn't recognize.

"Don't worry about Sam," Myrtle said, not even bothering to lower her voice. "He's gotten so deaf he wouldn't hear a firecracker if one went off under his chair. And the other old fellow, that's Gaylord Thornton, Isaac Easton's uncle. Isaac and the missus took Gaylord in a couple of years ago. Most of the time Gaylord can't remember his own name, but he sure hasn't forgotten how to play checkers. He and Sam get along fine. Gaylord's happy Sam's not always asking questions he can't remember the answers to, and Sam's happy he don't have to pretend he can hear."

Myrtle had been busy preparing Lottie's iced tea the entire time she was talking. Now she set the tall frosty glass in front of Lottie, adding a second sprig of fresh mint.

Lottie took a long slow swallow. "It's even better than I remember," she said, and was rewarded by Myrtle's smile.

"Fresh lemon, fresh mint and fresh-brewed tea. That's the secret. Never brew your tea and let it sit around all day. Now, about what you were asking—sure, there's been all kinds of talk—but none of it particularly mean-spirited, if you know what I mean. Heard you were fitting in just fine at the bank. Josephine Winters says you know what you're doing and that when you're in the teller's cage, your drawer balances to the penny. And Hiram says your account ledgers are meticulous. That's high praise from Hiram. You've got the members of the historical society on your side, too. They're delighted you're fixing up the Blackburn place. Even Mildred Gaston had a kind word."

Now that was welcome news, Lottie thought, even better than she'd dared hope. She took another sip of tea, knowing that her next question wouldn't be so easy. "What about my father? What do they say?" she finally asked.

"Well, of course, there's been talk," Myrtle said. "After all, it was a bona fide scandal. Even had the papers from Little Rock up here." She paused a moment. "How much of it did you know or do you remember?"

"What I didn't know then, I've read about," Lottie said. "I don't think there're any secrets."

"Then you had to realize it would all be resurrected," Myrtle said bluntly. "Funny thing, though. Lots of the stories I've heard repeated about your father have been good memories, about things that happened before the scandal. I've heard one or two suggestions that maybe he didn't really mean to keep the money, that he meant to turn it over to the bank all along. Even heard some speculation that maybe his death was an accident, not suicide. That maybe he'd gone up to the bluff to think and maybe the car accidentally rolled over the top."

Lottie shook her head. Wishful thinking. She'd given up such fairy tales long ago.

"I know," Myrtle said, "but what I'm trying to say is your family had a lot of friends in this town. Sometimes I think maybe your mother should've stuck it out."

"My mother never lost faith in my father. She was a strong woman in many ways, but she wasn't one to face down contempt. Or pity."

"Well, I guess there's no reason to waste time thinking about might-have-beens, anyway." Myrtle swiped the counter with the towel again. "Question now is, what are you going to do?"

"I came back," Lottie said, "and I plan to stay."

A wide grin spread across Myrtle's face. "That's what I wanted to hear."

WHEN HIS GRANDMOTHER first suggested he escort Lottie Carlyle to the annual Little Falls Founders Day celebrations, Harve said no. No equivocation. No ambiguity. Just a simple and articulate no.

Not only had he declined to accompany Lottie, he hadn't planned to attend at all. Yet here he was, only minutes away from Armageddon. Worse, he found himself torn between feelings of anticipation and trepidation.

He muttered a pithy oath under his breath and turned his truck onto the gravel driveway leading to the apartment at the back of his grandmother's house.

Dammit, anyway. He should have stuck to his original decision.

As if he'd had a choice. His grandmother had been determined, and a determined Abigail Tremayne was an unbeatable force.

She'd reminded him that the bank was one of the Founders Day sponsors and that Lottie, as the bank's new vice president, was expected to attend.

"It will be Charlotte's first official appearance in front of the entire community, and she'll need support," his grandmother had said. "She certainly won't receive it from Cyrus."

Abigail had also reminded him that at least one Tremayne should attend, then delivered her coup de grâce. "I've been carrying the family banner for the past several years, but this year I'm simply too old and too tired. You'll have to do it."

He'd experienced a moment of panic. Was his grandmother ill and hiding it from him? She was indomitable but not indestructible. She was also a master at converting him to her viewpoint, but never before had she resorted to using her age and frailty as a weapon against him.

Something of his thoughts must have shown on his face, because she'd quickly backtracked. "I assure you, Harvey, I am perfectly well, although I'll admit the idea of attending another Founders Day is daunting. I've attended so many, you see. But I suppose one more won't make much difference."

Harve had snorted. In the end he'd capitulated,

assuring his grandmother that he would attend. He knew it was a decision that was going to have far-reaching consequences.

Hadn't he spent the past few weeks carefully avoiding Lottie Carlyle? His campaign had been mostly successful, too, aided, he suspected, by the lady's similar goals.

Ah, hell. Who was he kidding? He might have been able to avoid seeing her, but she was never far from his thoughts. He couldn't seem to shake the memory of her surprise entrance into the boardroom. Even before he'd realized who she was, he'd suspected she could wreak havoc in his life. When she'd turned her gaze on him, meeting his questioning eyes without flinching, he'd felt his pulse quicken, like a racehorse about to spring from the starting gate.

He'd tried to tell himself that it meant nothing, that she'd merely caught him off guard. A knee-jerk reaction. Then he'd gone after her like a rooster chasing a hen and found that encounter no less disturbing than the first.

Their few subsequent meetings had done nothing to weaken the intensity of his reaction. Talk about understatement! They'd left him as frustrated as a stallion unable to get to a pasture full of mares.

What about Lottie? If she was trying to avoid him, as he suspected, she would be no more eager for this excursion than he. What arguments had his grandmother used to persuade her to accept his escort?

He sighed, a sound that was both bitter and resigned. As if he didn't know.

It had been five years since he'd last attended Founders Day—five years less one day since his fiancée, Rosemary, had died of a brain embolism. He could hear his grandmother now, arguing that Lottie would be doing him a favor by giving him an excuse to break his self-imposed boycott. He knew his grandmother believed he avoided the celebrations because it reminded him of the last time he and Rosemary were together.

It wasn't so. At least not entirely.

Oh, he'd admit he'd sleepwalked through that first year, wanting no reminders of the future fate had stolen from him. Maybe he'd even avoided the celebrations the next year for similar reasons, but he'd finally realized that Rosemary would want to be remembered with love, not grief, and been able to let her go. Since then, his avoidance of Founders Day was more habit than anything.

Until this year. This year he'd had a reason for not wanting to attend—namely, Lottie Carlyle. He didn't like his feelings of attraction, of vulnerability, when he was near her.

Harve turned off the truck and sat for a moment staring at Lottie's door. He felt like a bear that had been pulled from his hibernation before time—torn between retreating into his winter sanctuary and venturing forth into the bright world.

Harve had the distinct feeling it was too late for a retreat.

## CHAPTER FIVE

WHY HAD SHE AGREED to this?

Lottie glanced surreptitiously at her escort. Harve had been in a strange mood from the moment he'd picked her up at his grandmother's. Oh, he was courteous enough under that cloak of reserve he usually wore, but something in his demeanor made her wary.

Stealing a second look at him as he stood engrossed in conversation with a local beef rancher, she willed herself to control the flutter of her heart she felt whenever he was near. He was dressed in the Western wear he preferred—blue denim jeans and jacket, a muted plaid cowboy shirt complete with pearl-button snaps, hand-tooled cowboy boots and the ever-present Stetson, this time a dark gray. The jeans hugged his trim hips and long muscular legs; the jacket stretched across broad shoulders. *Every woman's dream cowboy!*

Her initial reaction to Abby's suggestion that Harve accompany her today had been anything but positive. But when Abby had told her about Rosemary, Lottie had experienced a rush of sympathy for Harve and a better understanding of that guarded look in his eyes. Agreeing with Abby's suggestion seemed little enough to do.

Still, she must be crazy. What had happened to her instincts for self-preservation?

Her plans to rescue the bank were only beginning to come together. Normally she'd want the board involved, but this time she believed that making her own decisions would serve her best. Harve had made no secret of his desire to know her rescue strategy, and although he hadn't yet reintroduced the subject, she was sure he would before the day was finished.

"Ms. Carlyle?"

Startled from her thoughts by the beef rancher's voice, Lottie desperately tried to remember the man's name. She should have been paying more attention when they were introduced. Darn it, anyway, why did she allow Harve to distract her this way? It was another reason to avoid him.

"I know today's not the right time to be discussing business, but I wonder if I might stop by the bank to see you sometime next week?"

"I'd be happy to see you, Mr. Jamison," she replied, relieved she'd managed to dredge his name from her memory.

"Tuesday morning?"

"That would be fine. I'll put you on my calendar." She gave him her best professional smile.

"Well, great," he said. "It's been real nice meeting you."

"Nice meeting you, too, Mr. Jamison. I'll look forward to Tuesday."

Lottie held her smile as she watched the rancher walk away, then turned to Harve. "Thank you for introducing us," she said. "It sounds as if he might be interested in bringing in some new business."

"Just doing my bit to support our mutual interests."

Her gaze met his. Had his offhand comment been intended as a reminder of his involvement in the bank? A signal that today's excursion was strictly business?

Probably, she decided. The thought should have reassured her. Strange that it did not.

"Jamison bought the old Hines place about six years ago," Harve added. "He runs a good operation, and although he's got a local account, he does most of his business out of town. He and Cyrus don't get along."

"Does anyone get along with Cyrus?" Lottie asked jokingly.

"Not many," he said. "I really am glad you decided to come back, Lottie. We both know the bank needs shaking up. Have you made any specific plans?"

Well, she'd known he would ask that question, hadn't she? "I've got a few ideas, but nothing definite yet," she said.

She barely managed to contain her surprise when he didn't press her for details.

"But you're not having any problems? Cyrus isn't putting any roadblocks in your way? Everyone's accepting your position?"

She thought briefly of the anonymous note, then dismissed it. That was two weeks ago, and there'd been nothing since. "About what I expected," she told him. "I'm keeping busy."

"Okay. Let me know if I can help." He hesitated a moment and looked about to say something else, then apparently changed his mind. She was relieved.

"So," he said, "what do you want to do now? We've got a choice of seeing quilt-making and home-canning exhibits in the exhibition hall or looking in on the junior rodeo."

"The rodeo," she said. "It's too nice a day to be inside."

His sudden infectious grin told her he seconded her choice. She found it impossible not to return that grin, even allowed herself a moment to bask in the warmth of his approval. Sometimes she wished—

Harve's hand curved around her elbow and her thoughts shattered into incoherent fragments. She could feel the burning imprint of his fingers and she stiffened. His hand fell abruptly away even as she realized his gesture had only been intended to guide her through the crowds toward the rodeo area.

Had he noticed her reaction?

*Don't be stupid,* she berated herself. Of course

he had. Why else would he have dropped her arm as though he'd been scalded?

She tried to force her confused emotions into order. Could she pretend it hadn't happened?

"Lead the way," she told him in a voice that sounded a little too bright and cheerful, then deliberately laid her hand on his arm. She caught the enigmatic look he threw her, but to her relief he didn't comment.

Founders Day dated from 1849 when the town's entire population of sixty-five had turned out to celebrate its first anniversary with a "schoolhouse raising." That one-room school still stood on Main Street and now served as headquarters and museum of the Little Falls Historical Society.

As the town grew so had the celebrations. By the time she was a teenager, the crowds at the event rivaled those at the high school's annual homecoming game in both size and enthusiasm.

Apparently not much had changed. In addition to the rodeo, a horseshoe-throwing competition and various local-crafts-judging contests, the schedule included three-legged and sack races, pie-eating contests and tonight's square-dancing competition.

"Is this how you remember it?" Harve asked as if he'd read her mind.

"Almost exactly," she said. "I'm a little surprised. I would have thought it would either have grown larger or withered away."

"Several years ago the town council talked about

trying to make it a more regional event," he told her. "Even went as far as discussing an independent Founders Day association to work with the state tourist bureau. But the community decided they didn't want a bunch of outsiders coming in and commercializing Founders Day."

"Which side were you on?"

He shrugged. "We kept the original community Founders Day. Still, the event could have put a lot of tourist dollars into local merchants' pockets. Without the merchants there won't be a Little Falls to commemorate Founders Day, and some of them have had rough times in recent years."

"It sounds as if you haven't made up your mind."

"I do have mixed feelings," he admitted. "There's no question that the downtown area needs a shot in the arm, but one weekend a year probably wouldn't help much, anyway."

Maybe her idea to start Saturday banking hours would help more than just the bank, Lottie thought. She wondered if the local merchants would be interested in cosponsoring an occasional Saturday promotional event. It was worth investigating at least.

As they neared the rodeo arena, the sounds of the public-address system and the cheers of the crowd pulled her from her thoughts.

"It seems we've arrived in time for the presentation of the court," Harve said. "Does it bring back memories? You were Rodeo Queen in 1984, weren't you?"

Lottie felt her throat tighten. "It was 1983."

"I was close. I remember it, though. There wasn't any question that you were the best rider in the court. You and that horse of yours were poetry in motion. I could never understand it. That horse— What did you call him?"

"Shyster." The name came out low and breathy. The memories and emotions caught her by surprise, and she struggled to keep her voice from breaking. "His name was Shyster."

"Right. I remember now. Big ugly brute. He was undoubtedly the sorriest specimen of horseflesh I've ever seen. Clumsy. Ungainly. Wrong proportions. Until you got on his back. Then he turned into a prince. Whatever happened to him, anyway?"

"I...I don't know."

"You don't..." His voice trailed into silence as he recognized her distress. "Lottie?" His tone was concerned, the expression on his face apologetic. "Oh, damn. I'm sorry. I didn't think—"

"No, it's all right." She took a deep breath, fighting for composure. "It's just...I haven't thought about Shyster in a long time."

"And I had to open my big mouth and—"

"I said it was all right, Harve. When we moved to Saint Louis, my mother sold him. She got an excellent price for him, so I'm sure he went to a good home. Besides, it was a long time ago, and I've got happy memories, too."

"I don't know if it'll help," Harve said, "but old Shyster did leave behind a kind of legacy."

"Legacy?" Lottie shook her head and grinned slightly. "That's impossible. I thought you were a horseman. Shyster was a gelding."

"Not that kind of legacy, squirt." His laughter rumbled from deep in his chest. "I do know the difference between a stud and a gelding." He hesitated a moment, as if lost in memory.

How could she have ever thought his eyes hard? They were as soft and blue as the sky on a misty summer morning. And he'd called her "squirt," the way he used to. Though she didn't like it any more now than she had when she was a kid, he'd said it with affection.

"I had a colt born on the farm several years ago," he continued. "Good bloodlines on both sides. He should have been a beau, but he was a sorry-looking thing, too. His conformation was a disaster. Even Harry, my barn manager, who's a tenderhearted marshmallow when it comes to his babies, urged me to get rid of him. For some reason I remembered that old horse of yours and I held on to him. I called him Rack 'n Ruin."

Harve turned to face Lottie and took her hands in his. Her breath caught in her throat.

"So what happened?"

"I sold him a few years ago to a young rodeo bum."

"And?"

"That rodeo bum was named national champion in the calf-roping competition at Madison Square Garden last year. He was riding Rack 'n Ruin."

Lottie blinked against the sudden moisture in her eyes and swallowed. Hard. "Thank you for telling me," she said finally.

"You're welcome," he said, the gentle smile on his lips setting her insides churning. As they stood holding hands, their surroundings, the shapes and noises around them, blurred like a fade-out scene in an old movie. Lottie was afraid to breathe, believing that even the slightest movement would shatter the illusion.

"Well, let's go look at this year's royalty," Harve said at last, breaking the spell. "See if any of them can live up to a certain predecessor I know."

She blinked again and gave herself a mental shake as Harve slipped one hand under her elbow. This time she didn't stiffen.

As they moved into the bleachers searching for seats she heard her name being called and recognized Jeff, waving from several rows above them.

"It's good to see you both here," her cousin said as they joined him. "Lottie, I'd like you to meet Jeannie, my wife."

The small woman standing at Jeff's side seemed

vagu~ly familiar, but Lottie was sure they'd never met.

Her hair was that color of red usually called strawberry blond, and her hazel eyes were wide and twinkling. She had freckles across the bridge of her pert upturned nose, and her generous mouth curved upward in a warm smile.

Lottie liked her immediately.

"I've been wanting to meet you," Jeannie said. "I hope we can be friends."

"I'd like that," Lottie told her. "I've wanted to meet you, too—and to thank you for organizing my office for me."

"I didn't do much," Jeannie said. "Just directed the grunt labor."

"I'm not sure I like being called grunt labor." Jeff's mock indignation made Lottie smile.

"Ladies and gentleman—" a hush settled over the crowd at the sound of expectancy in the announcer's voice "—may I present your new Junior Rodeo Queen, Miss Gayle Blackburn, riding King."

"She did it. Oh, Jeff, she did it!" Jeannie threw her arms around Jeff's neck, her squeal of delight all but drowning out the last part of the announcement.

Lottie's attention swung to the arena and the small figure sitting atop a big chestnut gelding—a figure that was unmistakably familiar. No braids today. Instead, her copper hair curled over her shoulders and down her back. There was no smudge of dirt on her cheek, either, and an elegant deep-fringed cowgirl outfit had replaced her muddy jeans and T-shirt. Lottie was too far away to see the freckles across the bridge of the girl's nose, but she knew they were there, exactly like her mother's. No wonder Jeannie had looked so familiar.

"Harve, that's the—"

"That's our daughter," Jeff said, his voice bursting with pride. He grinned. "Another Blackburn Rodeo Queen."

"I've seen—" Lottie stopped abruptly, remembering how the girl had begged her not to tell anyone. As well, there was a look of apprehension and pleading in Jeannie's eyes. Did Jeannie know about her daughter's secret gardening activities? If so, she apparently didn't want it mentioned, either. Didn't Jeff know? "I've never seen a prettier Rodeo Queen," she amended hastily, and saw the relief cross Jeannie's face.

"She's a good little rider," Jeff boasted. "Takes after her mother that way. She sure didn't get it from me."

Lottie couldn't help but laugh. Jeff's distinct lack of riding skills was well-known and much chronicled in family circles.

After the presentation of the rest of the court, they settled back in their seats to watch the rodeo. Lottie found herself enjoying Jeannie's company as much as the show. It was late afternoon when they finally said goodbye, but only after Jeannie had extracted a promise from Lottie to meet for lunch one day next week.

Lottie watched her cousin and his wife walk away, then turned to Harve. "You knew the girl in the rose garden was Jeff's daughter, didn't you?" she accused.

He shrugged. "I thought it probably was, but I wasn't positive. Besides, as I told you before, you were sure to see her sooner or later. I was right, wasn't I?"

The expression on his face wasn't exactly arrogant, she decided. It was more just...confident, as if he was so used to being right it was beyond his comprehension to entertain thoughts of being wrong. She gave him her best disgruntled look and shook her head.

What was it about him that made her itch to deflate his ego? A holdover from earlier times when she'd unconsciously challenged him to demand his attention? Surely she'd outgrown such tactics....

Shortly after midnight Harve drove Lottie back to his grandmother's farm. She felt relaxed and happy. Even the memory of a chance run-in with Uncle Cyrus failed to diminish her good mood. She'd enjoyed the day.

Had Harve?

She glanced over at him and saw that his lips were curved in a slight smile.

She'd admit the first few minutes of the day had

been awkward. For both of them. But it hadn't been long before they'd been joking and laughing together in the easy way of old friends.

It was he, in fact, who'd suggested they stay after the official activities ended and attend the dance in the high-school gym.

Several area fiddlers, already in place from the just-completed square-dance competition, had been joined on stage by the high-school band director Joe Treadway on an electronic keyboard and barbershop owner Charlie Zimmermann on base.

The band's repertoire was lively and varied but with a decidedly country-and-western flavor. The last number of the evening had been slow, and she'd fit into Harve's arms perfectly, just the right height to lay her cheek against his shoulder. She'd been thinking about that when, halfway through the song, he'd tightened his embrace and pulled her closer, almost as if he'd been reading her mind again. For the remaining couple of minutes she'd relaxed against him and allowed her fantasies free reign.

The change in the momentum of the truck as Harve turned onto the graveled driveway that led to Abby's shook her from her reverie. He drove around to the back of the house, parking the truck under the gas yard light and turned off the engine.

Lottie released her seat belt and turned to face him. "I had fun today," she blurted, suddenly as nervous as a teenager on a first date. "Thank you for taking me."

"I had fun, too. Thank you for going with me," he answered solemnly.

He caught and held her gaze, the expression in his eyes immobilizing her like a deer caught in headlights. What was happening to her? Did he feel it, too? Finally she managed to turn away and fumble with the door release.

"Just a minute," he commanded, unfastening his own seat belt.

"You don't need to get out," she protested, anxious now to put distance between them. "I can manage."

"I don't know how they do it in Saint Louis," he drawled, "but around here, when a fellow brings a girl home, he walks her to the door. It's tradition."

She nodded slowly, reluctant to concede defeat. "Just don't slam the truck door," she told him, trying to justify her actions. "I don't want to wake up Abby."

He grinned. "I'll be quiet," he said, "but it won't make any difference. If grandmother's asleep, nothing short of Grant attacking Richmond will wake her, and if she's awake, waiting to see what time I bring you home, there's no way we can be quiet enough. Besides, she'd have seen the truck lights coming up the driveway."

Harve eased himself off the seat, then closed the

truck door with no more than a barely audible click. Lottie turned away, staring straight ahead as Harve walked to the passenger-side door. She let him help her from the truck, giving a quick breath of relief when his touch fell away from her arm as soon as her feet were on the ground. She stepped back as he closed the passenger door, again with only the slightest of sounds.

He grinned, a teasing twist of the lips that reminded her of a mischievous little boy, then motioned for her to proceed him and fell into step behind her. Although it was only a short distance from the truck to the apartment door, Lottie felt as if she'd walked a mile. She dug into her purse for the key, then turned to face him.

"I really did have a good time today, Harve," she said carefully. "Thank you for asking me."

"You and I both know it was my grandmother's idea." His tone was wry. "She probably bamboozled you into going with me, but for once I'm glad she interfered. I'm glad I went, and I'm glad you agreed to go with me."

He paused, then said, "You know, there's another part to that tradition."

"What tradition?"

"The one about the fellow walking the girl to the door." He moved closer.

"Oh. That tradition." She retreated a step.

"Once the fellow has walked the girl to her door, he gets to claim a good-night kiss."

Was he teasing? His voice *sounded* as if he was teasing, but there was something about the expression in his eyes that said otherwise. "Harve, I don't think—"

"You wouldn't want to flout tradition, would you, Ms. Carlyle?"

Before she could form a response, Harve had caught her chin with one hand, tipped her face up and lowered his head. He seemed to hesitate for a moment, as if giving her a last chance for protest, then brought his mouth to hers.

It began as a gentle kiss, feather soft, warm, inviting. And so exactly right. Her lips opened under his like the petals of a morning glory opening to the rays of the sun.

He gave a groan and deepened the kiss—no gentle caress now, but a searing assault on her senses that left her reeling.

Heaven help her! She'd been right to be wary. This was a mistake. Even as the notion formed, it dissolved, lost in the tingling electricity of her response.

Then, as abruptly as he'd begun, he ended the kiss, stepping back, his eyes searching her face. "Good night, Lottie," he said, his voice thick and unsteady, and turned to walk toward the truck.

"Good night," she answered weakly as she watched him walk away.

HARVE GRIPPED the steering wheel, his knuckles white, as he fought the urge to speed down the driveway.

He'd made a mistake! No simple mistake, either, but one great colossal blunder.

He shouldn't have touched her. He certainly shouldn't have kissed her.

As he turned the truck onto the highway and accelerated, a deep sound, something between a sigh and a snort of disgust, rumbled from his throat. *As if putting distance between us will erase my actions!* he thought, and slowed to a more respectable speed. It was also impossible, he knew, to outrun his thoughts.

He'd only meant to give her a good-night peck, one of those generic thank-you-for-sharing-a-good-time-with-me kisses. Okay, he'd admit it. He'd kissed her on a teasing impulse. At least, that was how it had started. They'd both been uneasy when he'd picked her up this morning, but the initial awkwardness between them had quickly faded. Then, when he'd gotten her home, she'd turned all tense and jumpy again.

What had she expected him to do? Try to get her into bed?

Her behavior had pricked his pride and he'd decided to teach her a lesson. So what had he done?

He'd kissed her—just a simple, run-of-the-mill, happens-every-day kind of kiss.

Yeah, right. And pigs could fly.

His emotional response to her had never been passive, he realized. Surprise, anger, annoyance, joy, confidence, irritation, she'd been able to invoke them all in him, even as a child. Unbidden came the memory of his last high-school track meet. He'd rounded the final turn in third place, his lungs bursting, his legs pumping but leaden, his vision of the finish line blurred. Somehow he'd heard one distinctive voice above the yells and cheers of the boisterous crowd. "Run, Harve! Come on! You can do it!"

His breathing had suddenly become easier, his legs lighter, and with that voice ringing in his ears, he'd crossed the finish line half a stride in front of his nearest opponent.

Had he realized then it was Lottie's voice urging him on? Probably not. Or maybe he had and simply never consciously acknowledged it.

Just as he'd refused to acknowledge the awareness that flared between them even on that first day she'd returned to town.

He'd loved Rosemary with a deep quiet emotion that soothed the empty places in his life. He'd mourned her with a grief intensified by the realization that fate, not will, controlled his future.

Since Rosemary's death, he'd enjoyed female companionship, but only on a casual basis. The encounters had been infrequent, no real emotion involved on either side.

And he'd been content.

Had he subconsciously known that a relationship with Lottie could never be casual? Was that why he'd been so determined to keep his distance?

Sure it was. Casual was safe.

What was he thinking? Dammit, he should have left well enough alone. The last thing he needed was to get involved with Lottie Carlyle.

He still didn't know if she'd returned to Little Falls for good. Or what plans she was making at the bank. If she'd made any, she was certainly keeping them to herself.

He was in trouble here. He'd been in trouble since she'd looked at him across the boardroom table.

That was before he'd kissed her.

Before she'd responded.

Before his world had tilted on its axis.

Oh, Lord. What was he supposed to do now?

## CHAPTER SIX

ONE MORE TIME, Lottie told herself as she hit the advance key on the computer and slowly scrolled through the investment accounts. Figures danced in columns down the page—precise, balanced, exactly as expected. The interest rate, the return on investments, was ridiculously low, but she'd already known that.

So why did that nagging little voice in the back of her mind keep telling her she was missing something?

Oh, all right. She'd admit it. Her subconscious knew her concentration had gone south and was warning her to pay attention to what she was doing.

It was all Harve's fault. Ever since...ever since he'd kissed her. It had been nothing but a friendly good-night kiss between old friends, she reminded herself. Okay, very friendly. So what if her knees had gone weak and she'd heard birds singing in the middle of the night?

Darn him, anyway. He'd kissed her until her toenails curled, then said good-night and walked away. It hadn't meant a thing, not to him. If she required proof of that, all she needed to do was look at the calendar. The day after tomorrow was Saturday. It was almost a week since he'd kissed her—almost a week since she'd even seen him.

Wasn't that what she wanted? Hadn't she been telling herself, since the first day she'd returned to Little Falls, that she needed to avoid Harve Tremayne? So why was she sitting here feeling sorry for herself?

She made a sound of disgust. Enough was enough. This wasn't the first time she'd been attracted to a man who had no interest in her.

Heck, this wasn't even the first time she'd been attracted to this particular man.

Ironic, wasn't it?

No, pitiful.

Well, no more. She'd returned to Little Falls to try to save the family bank, not to moon after Harvey Tremayne. It was time she got on with it.

Tomorrow she'd fire the first salvo in her battle to increase the customer base by announcing plans for Saturday-morning business hours. For a time she'd be too busy implementing and defending her decision to give Harve Tremayne a thought. That was exactly as it should be.

Satisfied with her conclusions, she looked at her watch, then turned off her computer. Today was the day she'd arranged to meet Jeannie Blackburn for lunch.

Minutes later she walked into the Down Home and spotted Jeannie already sitting at a table in the back of the room. She maneuvered her way across the crowded café to Jeannie, who greeted her with a smile. "Thank you for agreeing to see me today," the woman said.

"Thank you for inviting me," Lottie said, seating herself. "I was glad for an excuse to get out of the bank for a little while."

"I especially wanted to thank you for not mentioning that Gayle had been working in the rose garden," Jeannie said next. "Jeff didn't know about it."

Lottie frowned. "So I gathered, but I don't understand why. Would he really object?"

"Yes. No, not really. I mean..." Jeannie sighed. "It's a complicated story."

"Hey, Jeannie, Lottie, what can I get you?" Myrtle interrupted.

"The special sounds good," Lottie told her, "with iced tea."

"Make it two," Jeannie said.

Lottie waited until Myrtle had moved toward the counter, then turned her attention back to Jeannie. "What do you mean?"

Jeannie twisted her hands together. "A couple of years ago it was obvious that your house was deteriorating badly," she said. "Jeff went in and did some emergency repairs on the roof. He said...he said it was his ancestral home, too." Jeannie delivered this last in a voice that alternated between defense and apology.

Lottie nodded. "Go on," she prompted.

Apparently encouraged by Lottie's failure to take offense, Jeannie stopped twisting her hands. "He contacted your mother, volunteered to do some additional maintenance and told her he was interested in buying the house if she was planning to sell."

Lottie hadn't known of the offer, but she knew what her mother's response would have been. "And Mother refused," she said bluntly.

"Worse than that," Jeannie said. "She had her attorney contact Jeff and inform him that if he so much as stepped foot on her property, she'd have him arrested for trespassing."

"Oh, no," Lottie moaned. "I'm sorry, Jeannie."

"It wasn't your fault," Jeannie said, "but it made Jeff furious. Gayle and I had been working in the rose garden while Jeff worked on the roof. Of course, after your mother's notice, he said the house could fall down as far as he was concerned. He didn't mean it, I don't think, but he expressly forbade Gayle to go back over there."

Jeannie shrugged and held up her hands in a gesture of helplessness. "The garden was already in bad shape. Weeds had almost choked out several beds. All the plants needed pruning and thinning, and several were infested with black spot. Anyway, Gayle was determined to save them. Or at least try. She disobeyed her father and snuck off to work in the garden.

"I didn't know what she was doing at first,"

Jeannie went on, "and when I found out, well, I simply 'forgot' to mention it to Jeff. I've told him now of course...."

"I'm so sorry," Lottie told her. "All I can say is that my mother wasn't always so...unreasonable. I can't tell you how glad I am that your daughter took care of the rose garden. When I saw how Mother had let the house deteriorate, I was afraid the garden would be in the same shape and that some of early species had been lost forever. It was a wonderful surprise to step around the hedge and see what I saw. For a moment I thought I was hallucinating."

Lottie reached across the table to squeeze Jeannie's hand. "I certainly wouldn't encourage your daughter to disobey her parents, but in this case, I'm sure glad she did."

"Is this the time to admit I stole a couple of cuttings?" Jeannie asked.

Lottie laughed. "Again, I'm glad. In fact, we should take several from a couple of the specimens. They can't be replaced."

By the time Myrtle served their meals, they were talking like old friends. Or relatives, Lottie thought. For a long time her mother had been her only family. She was glad she and Jeannie seemed to be kindred spirits. Family was important. It felt good to have one again.

FRIDAY MORNING at nine-forty-five Lottie walked into the conference room and stationed herself at the head of the table. She'd worn her red suit this morning—for confidence. And she'd deliberately called the all-bank personnel meeting for this time, wanting the announcement to be a complete surprise and hoping the timing would limit the opportunity for discussion and argument.

She had to present Cyrus with a fait accompli. Otherwise he'd try to block her. She'd win in the end, but the bank couldn't afford the scars of a public battle. Neither could it afford the delay. If she was going to save the bank, every day was crucial.

Jefferson was the question mark. After working with him on a daily basis she realized he wasn't as reactionary as his father, but she also had firsthand knowledge of how he reacted to surprises. The best she could hope for was that he'd exercise discretion until after the meeting.

Cyrus was the first to enter the room. "What do you mean calling a meeting at this time of the day?" he demanded. "Our doors open in less than fifteen minutes."

"I have a short announcement to make, Uncle Cyrus," she told him. "Since it affects everyone, I felt it only fair that everyone hear it at the same time."

Emma Whitehall snorted. "So you're leaving already," she said, disdain in her voice. "Figured you wouldn't be here long."

Lottie shook her head. "Sorry to disappoint you, Emma, but I'm here to stay."

She glanced around the room, doing a mental head count, then nodded when Hiram, the bookkeeper, slipped in the door.

"I won't keep you more than a minute," she said, "but I wanted to announce that, beginning Saturday, two weeks from tomorrow, the Little Falls Bank will be opening from ten to noon. The decision to expand banking hours is being made for customer convenience and in an effort to make us more competitive with other financial institutions in the area. Letters to our bank customers will be mailed today, and an announcement will be appearing in Monday's edition of the *Little Falls Gazette*. Notices are also being placed in other area newspapers next week. I realize this—"

"Now, wait just a minute," Cyrus protested.

"Let me finish, Uncle Cyrus, then you can have your say. As you reminded me a moment ago, we open in a very few minutes."

She pointedly returned her attention to the others in the room. "As I was saying, I realize this action is going to require some shuffling of work schedules. I'll be addressing those concerns with each of you personally in the next few days. In the meantime I wanted to inform you before you heard it on the grapevine."

A glance around the conference room confirmed

that she'd caught them all by surprise, but only Cyrus's and Emma's faces indicated disapproval.

"How dare you—" Cyrus began, his complexion purple with rage.

"It was a decision that needed to be made," she said firmly. "I made it."

She looked at her wristwatch. "Heads up, everyone. Doors open in five minutes. We'll talk more later."

She watched as Hiram, Josephine and Emma left the room. Jeff seemed to hesitate a moment, looking anxiously from her to his father.

"I'll get the doors," he told Cyrus, then followed the others out of the room.

Lottie turned to her uncle. "The decision is final, Uncle Cyrus, but if you like, I'll be glad to discuss my reasons with you."

"The board won't allow—"

"Operations, including the setting of banking hours, is a prerogative of the bank's officers, not the board. I haven't publicly claimed the title of chief executive officer, but I will if necessary. I have the authority," she reminded him.

She wished she could have read his thoughts. Was he furious because she'd outmaneuvered him by making a unilateral decision, or was it typical Blackburn stubbornness and his innate resistance to change?

Both, probably. She knew that making the announcement without consulting him first was not good management, but had she really had a choice? If she'd tried to discuss it with him beforehand, he would have objected, and his opposition would only have caused division among bank personnel.

"I'm sorry I didn't consult you before the announcement," she told him, "but we both know you would have fought me, and quite frankly we can't afford the time for an argument. For many different reasons our customer base has been shrinking for years. More convenient banking hours are only a partial remedy, but an easy and quick one."

"Our bank has always served its customers well, better than any of those big faceless banks. Our customers know it. They're loyal," he said.

"Yes, they are," she agreed, "but hometown loyalty can only stretch so far. Adding Saturday hours won't affect our current loyal customers, but it'll be more convenient for some and may allow others who've had to change banks to come back."

The mutinous expression on his face didn't soften, but at least his high color was beginning to fade.

"We need more customers, a broader customer base," she said in a conciliatory tone. "I'm hoping to recapture some of our old customers, maybe even pick up some newer residents of the area. We need them, Uncle Cyrus. After nearly 150 years, I don't want to see this bank close its doors. I don't think you do, either."

"Of course I don't."

"Then support me. Let's try the Saturday hours. See if it helps."

"Banking days are Monday through Friday," he huffed. "Always have been. This customer-convenience stuff is nothing but a bunch of new-fangled falderal. You mark my words—only difference it's going to make is to disrupt a lot of people's weekends."

"I think you're wrong, Uncle Cyrus. I hope you are—not to best you in an argument, but because whether you admit it or not, the bank's in trouble. We have to turn things around. Expanded hours are a start."

"Time will tell who's right," he said, and stomped out of the room.

Why was she disappointed? Lottie wondered. What tiny bit of cockeyed optimism had allowed her to hope Cyrus would back her? Expanded banking hours was so obvious a solution to some of their problems he should have instigated them years ago.

She couldn't help wondering why he hadn't. Cyrus was a solid, if somewhat old-fashioned banker, who'd guided the bank through some perilous waters in the past. Even allowing that he was unimaginative and stubborn, it sometimes seemed he was determined to let the bank fail, rather than admit things had to change. That was what she couldn't understand. Or forgive.

Lottie returned to her office and began reviewing

files. A couple of hours later Jeff tapped on her open door.

"Here," he said, handing her a large brown manila envelope. "It's a plan for juggling work schedules to cover Saturday hours. If you and I each work an hour for Josephine, maybe on Wednesdays and Thursdays, then she can put in two hours on Saturday without going into overtime. The three of us should be able to handle Saturday mornings, and we won't have to disturb Hiram's schedule, or Dad's or Emma's. That should cover us, temporarily, anyway."

Lottie looked up at him with a puzzled frown. "You haven't had time to put this together since the meeting this morning," she said.

"I suggested Saturday hours last year," he told her. "Dad wouldn't even consider it and I didn't have the power to implement it. You do. After your meeting this morning I simply revised my earlier plan by adding your name to the schedule."

"Thanks, Jeff. I appreciate your support."

He shrugged. "We're in the same leaky boat, whether Dad'll admit it or not," he said. "Incidentally, if business picks up enough so that we need additional help, Jeannie's worked in a bank before. She might come in, off the clock, to cover phones and a few things like that. If we can hold it together until the end of summer, then Sally Flynn, who used to be our head teller, may be available part-time in September. That's when her twin boys start kindergarten.''

"That's good to know."

He nodded. "We're on the same side here, Lottie. I'm sorry Dad's giving you such a hard time. I think you're doing a good job, and if there's anything I can do to help, let me know."

In spite of Cyrus's anticipated opposition, Lottie viewed the rest of the day as positive. Jeff's attitude was an unanticipated plus. Josephine willingly agreed to the adjusted work schedule. Even Emma's sour comment that she, for one, did not intend to work on Saturday, failed to dampen Lottie's spirits, especially since she hadn't planned or wanted Emma's presence.

Tom Jamison was in to sign final papers on the farm-improvement loan they'd negotiated earlier in the week. The rancher planned to convert sixty acres of bottom land to alfalfa, and the loan included funds to cover anticipated loss of revenue from reducing his herd while the pasture was out of production, as well as the cost of a portable above-ground irrigation system.

Cyrus, Lottie knew, would not have approved the loan, because the home farm, which included the sixty acres, was already mortgaged, but she accepted a second piece of land, owned free and clear by the rancher, as security against the loan. It was a safe and accepted banking practice, and although Cyrus didn't like it, he couldn't protest her actions.

So all in all a good day, she decided, good enough to treat herself to an old-fashioned ice-cream soda at the Down Home before driving out to Abby's.

The bell over the door jingled merrily as she entered the café and nearly bumped into Tom Jamison.

"Good afternoon again, Ms. Carlyle," he said. "I've been telling everyone what a fine job you did for me on that loan."

"Why thank you, Mr. Jamison," Lottie replied. "We like satisfied customers. It's a pleasure doing business with you."

"I'm sure we'll be doing more business together," he said, then tugged at the brim of his Stetson.

Lottie was still grinning when she slipped into the only vacant seat at the counter. Apparently she and Mr. Jamison weren't the only ones who'd decided to finish the workweek at the Down Home.

Myrtle, dressed as always in her too-tight truckstop waitress uniform, bustled between counter and tables, carrying trays of coffee, soft drinks and pie. She waved at Lottie and called a "Be with you in a minute" greeting from the other end of the counter.

"Take your time," Lottie called back.

She glanced around the crowded café, pleased at the number of faces she could identify. A month ago, when she'd first returned to Little Falls, some faces might have seemed vaguely familiar, but she wouldn't have been able to attach names to them. Now she recognized feed-store owner Jacob Calley, eating pie with Andrew Pettigrew, the bank board member who, along with Abigail Tremayne, had officially supported her during that first board meeting. Charlie Zimmermann, obviously taking a break from his barbershop, was having a cup of coffee at the other end of the counter.

In fact, she realized, she had a speaking acquaintance with most of the town's businessmen now. They were in and out of the bank on an almost daily basis.

Across the room she saw Mildred Gaston, president of Little Falls Historical Society, deep in conversation with Emma Whitehall. Sam Taylor and Gaylord Thompson were at their usual table in back, and they continued to play checkers, oblivious to the chatter around them.

Myrtle set the coffeepot on the warmer, then moved to Lottie's end of the counter. "Afternoon, Lottie. What can I get you today?"

"Do you still make old-fashioned ice-cream sodas?"

"What kind of crazy question is that? Do dogs still bark?" She slapped her hand on the counter. "This here's a soda fountain, isn't it? Of course, I still make ice-cream sodas. Don't know if I'd call them old-fashioned, though. Just fattening."

Lottie grinned.

"So what's your flavor? Chocolate, vanilla, strawberry or cherry?"

"Cherry, please."

"Double or triple scoop?"

"Make it a triple."

"Atta girl."

As Myrtle moved to the freezer, Mildred Gaston passed by, giving Lottie a brief good-afternoon on her way out the door. Emma, following in her wake, didn't bother to speak.

"Don't let Emma get you down," Myrtle said as she set Lottie's ice-cream soda in front of her. "Eventually she'll come round."

"I'm not holding my breath," Lottie said with a sigh. "Sometimes I think she's even more antagonistic than Cyrus. I don't understand what I've done to her to make her dislike me so."

"I don't think it's anything you've done," Myrtle told her. "It's only that she's completely loyal to Cyrus. Has been since he went against his daddy and hired her. Win Cyrus's support and you'll win hers, too."

"Cyrus bucked my grandfather to hire her? I never knew that. Why on earth would grandfather object to Emma working at the bank?" Lottie asked as she ran a finger down the outside of the tall frosted soda glass.

"Well, now, that's another story. Goes back another generation. Emma's mother accused your great-granddaddy of stealing her bank shares. I've never heard Emma say anything about it, but I guess the old man was afraid she agreed with her mother."

"Wait a minute," Lottie said. "You mean Emma owned bank shares? How?"

"It wasn't Emma, it was her mother who owned the shares. She was some kind of shirttail kin to the Blackburns. Anyway, she inherited several shares from her grandfather, but in those days, a woman's place was in the home, not business. Way I heard the story, her father controlled the shares until she married, then her husband took over. Peyton Whitehall, that was Emma's father, wasn't interested in banking, and he sold his wife's shares to your great-granddaddy."

Myrtle lowered her voice to almost a whisper. "I suspect there wouldn't have been a problem, except old Peyton didn't bother to tell his wife he'd sold them and she didn't find out until after he'd up and disappeared, leaving her and Emma, who was just a kid at the time, to fend for themselves. Emma's mother sued your great-granddaddy for the shares and the courts found in his favor.

"Later, after Emma was grown and wanted to go work at the bank, your granddaddy said no. He didn't want a Whitehall in his bank. Cyrus hired her over his objections. Guess she's been working for him since before you were born."

"I never knew that," Lottie said. "No wonder she's so loyal to Cyrus. Maybe you're right. If I can convince Cyrus I know what I'm doing, I can win her over, too."

"Well, now, I don't know about Cyrus, but you've sure got some new fans with your Saturday-morning banking hours."

Lottie's mouth gaped. "How do you do it, Myrtle? How do you know what's happening in this town before it even happens? We're not publicly announcing the new hours until Monday."

Myrtle laughed. "Never you mind, Lottie Carlyle. Just don't underestimate the Little Falls grapevine. Incidentally, the town's business folk are delighted with the new hours. Claim it'll improve their Saturday business, too. Jamison was in here praising you to the stars for approving his loan. You're making progress, girl."

"I hope so."

"Oh, you just wait and see," Myrtle replied with a knowing wink.

## CHAPTER SEVEN

MAYBE HE SHOULD HAVE called first, Harve thought as he parked the truck at the back of his grandmother's house by Lottie's apartment.

No. He'd made the right decision. She'd be surprised to find him on her doorstep this morning. Almost as surprised as he was to find himself here. Besides, it would be harder for her to refuse him face-to-face than over the phone.

Ah, hell. Even as he tried to convince himself that staying in contact with her was his only chance to discover what she was doing at the bank, he knew he was kidding himself again.

He'd known that when he'd said goodbye last Saturday night. In fact, he'd have been on her doorstep the next day if he hadn't been scheduled to fly to Denver. And the bank had little to do with it.

Then his planned two-day trip had stretched into six. First he'd waited for parts to repair his ailing plane engine, then for a spring storm to clear the area.

He could no longer deny there was something special between them. How special he wasn't sure, but he was going to find out. Had she missed him as much as he'd missed her? Probably not. Damn, he felt like a high-school kid trying to gather his courage to ask a girl to the prom.

*Nothing ventured, nothing gained,* he reminded himself as he eased himself out of the truck. Moments later he was knocking on her door.

THE LAST PERSON Lottie expected to see standing on her porch stoop early Saturday morning was Harve Tremayne.

As she opened the door, he pushed the brim of his battered Stetson to the back of his head. Dressed in a shirt so old and faded that the original plaid was only a suggestion of interwoven colors, he looked nothing like a successful business entrepreneur. His shirt was tucked into a pair of equally ancient jeans. And his boots—they were run over at the heels and so scuffed she'd swear they hadn't seen polish since before she was born.

Yet one look at him was enough to undo an entire week of trying to convince herself she wasn't attracted to Harve Tremayne.

"What are you... I mean why—"

"Good morning, Lottie," he said. As his mouth curved into a smile, her heart rate accelerated.

*There ought to be a law against a man looking this good so early in the morning, especially dressed as he is—like an out-of-work cowboy.*

Her confusion was replaced by a sudden flash of anger. *After kissing me silly, then ignoring me all week, how dare he show up on my doorstep looking so calm and confident!*

"I wondered if you'd like to go horseback riding with me."

It was the last thing she'd expected him to say, and he'd said it as casually as anyone else might say "Nice weather we're having."

"Horseback riding? Now? You mean me?"

The laugh lines around his eyes crinkled as he looked over his shoulder before swinging his gaze back to her. "What's wrong with now? It's a beautiful spring morning, and of course I mean you. Do you see anyone else around?"

"But I haven't been on a horse in thirteen years," she protested.

"So?"

She gave him a look of exasperation. "Harve—" she struggled to keep her tone as patient as what she'd use with a three-year-old "—anyone who knows anything about horses knows Tremayne Farm raises some of the best quarter horses in the country. Your stock is registered, bonded and insured. Every hoof is worth hundreds, probably thousands, of dollars. And you're asking me, who hasn't been on a horse in years, if I want to go riding? Have you lost your mind?"

"Hey, I'm not suggesting a three-day equestrian event," he said. His deep laugh continued to do weird things to her pulse. "Just an easy morning ride. I've got a little mare who's perfect for you. I thought…well, I thought you might enjoy the outing. Fresh air, exercise. Be good for you after being cooped up in the bank all week. I realize you haven't been on a horse in a while, but it's like riding a bicycle. Once you know how, you don't forget. Besides,'' he added, "the mare needs the exercise and she's too small for my weight."

"Ah, now we come to the truth. You just need an exercise boy."

"I have exercise boys," he said bluntly. "I'd rather ride with you."

The intense expression in his eyes made a shiver skitter up her spine. Instinct cautioned her to say no. Emotion told her to say yes. "I don't have riding boots," she told him, a last-ditch attempt to resist the irresistible.

"My cousin left a pair at the house. They should fit you. If not, any sturdy shoes will do."

She hesitated another moment, then gave in. "All right," she said. "If you're sure you want to trust me on one of your horses…"

He grinned and the fine squint lines around his eyes reappeared. "I'd trust you on any horse in my stable," he said, and her heart rate accelerated again. "You may be a little rusty, but I remember how well you used to ride. All you need is to get back in practice."

His praise sent a wave of pleasure surging through her. "I have a feeling my muscles may not agree with you tonight," she told him. "It's going to take more than a little practice to get this body used to riding again.''

She swallowed as his gaze swept over her—from head to toe, then back again. ''I don't see a thing wrong with that body,'' he said, ''but if you're worried about aches and pains, I have a remedy. Bring a swimsuit and we'll hit the hot tub after our ride. You'd better bring a jacket, too. It's cool this morning.''

He waited while she changed into a pair of jeans and dug an old pair of hiking boots from the back of the closet.

''So how did your week go?'' he asked after she climbed into the truck for the short ride to his ranch.

''You don't know? You must have missed yesterday's visit to the Down Home.''

He threw her an enigmatic look. ''As a matter of fact, I missed all last week. Got stranded in Denver. I didn't get in until late last night. Didn't Grandmother tell you?''

''No, she didn't mention it.'' He'd been in Denver all week! He hadn't been deliberately avoiding her!

''So what have I missed?''

''Not a lot,'' she said, ''but I've decided to start opening the bank on Saturday mornings. The official announcement won't be made until Monday, but you know Little Falls. The word's already out.''

''What does Cyrus have to say?''

''He's against it of course. I overrode him.''

"Atta girl. For what it's worth, I approve. Every bank in the area but ours opens on Saturdays. When do you start?"

"Two weeks from today. So far, the feedback's been positive. At least, the business community seems to approve."

"You don't waste time once you make up your mind, do you?" He grinned, but somehow she managed to keep her pulse at an acceptable speed.

"We don't have much time," she said.

His grin faded. "No, I don't guess we do. But Saturday hours may bring in new customers."

"I hope so," she said.

"Are you planning anything else? What about the bank's investment portfolio?"

"I'm still studying it," she replied, stalling.

He looked as if he wanted to ask something else, then apparently changed his mind. "Well, if there's anything I can do..."

"Keep your fingers crossed and your money in the bank," she said lightly, hoping he'd drop the subject.

"Done. If you need it, I'll hold your hand, too."

Her throat tightened. "I'll remember that."

THE LITTLE MARE was everything he'd promised—sleek and frisky, but well mannered and possessed of a smooth gait.

They rode for a little over an hour, crisscrossing pastures and winding up on the trail that led up

Tremayne Mountain. At that point Harve announced they'd ridden long enough for her first outing.

Lottie wanted to protest, but bit her tongue. She wasn't sure whom she was more annoyed with, Harve or herself.

Darn it, anyway. During the past few weeks she'd begun to believe he'd changed his bossy "I know best" ways. She should have known he'd revert to form.

But didn't the ache in her legs and the twinge of pain in her back tell her he was right? Her desire to protest, then, was a carryover, she supposed, from the days when she challenged him constantly in her efforts to draw his attention.

*So grow up, Lottie,* she told herself.

When they arrived back at the barn, she insisted on unsaddling and rubbing down her mount.

"I rode her. I'll take care of her," she said, despite his assurance that a stableboy would handle it. She also declined the use of the hot tub and asked him to take her back to Abby's. She planned to spend the day working at her house in town. Although Abby's hospitality was impeccable, she was anxious to move to her own place.

"You can ride whenever you find time," Harve told her. "I'll leave word at the barn. Two or three short rides a week and you'll be back in shape in no time."

Even as she thanked him, she knew she wouldn't

be taking him up on his offer. This morning had been an unplanned event, a temptation she'd been unable to refuse, although she'd known it wasn't wise. Besides, between the bank and the restoration work at her house, there didn't seem to be enough hours in the day.

*Stay focused. Harve's a distraction you can't afford,* she reminded herself.

She showered quickly, then drove into town. The house was looking better every day. The porch banisters and corner braces had been repaired, and most of the exterior had been scraped and was now awaiting fresh paint. A new electrical circuit-breaker box had been installed on the back porch.

Although she'd received permission from Jeannie and Jeff for young Gayle to continue caring for the rose garden, the rest of the yard was still a disaster. She itched to have the yard restored to its former beauty, but told herself that chore could wait. A livable house was her first priority.

Her objective for the day was to clean and polish the kitchen cabinets. Handcrafted from American chestnut, a native hardwood no longer available, the cabinets were part of the charm of the old house, as well as an irreplaceable piece of history.

Why, she wondered again, had her mother so completely abandoned the place? She could understand the bitterness toward the townsfolk, but the house had been not only her mother's childhood home, but a place of happiness during her marriage and Lottie's childhood. Hadn't that alone made it worth preserving?

Lottie worked until early evening, delaying her return to Abby's until she feared the woman would begin to worry about her absence. With her spirits buoyed by her day's accomplishment, she decided to return to the old house the next day.

She attended church Sunday morning, then excused herself from joining Abby for lunch and hurried to town. She was stripping old wallpaper in an upstairs bedroom when the clang of the old-fashioned front doorbell echoed through the empty house. But if she was surprised to hear the bell ring, she was even more surprised to see Harve standing on the porch.

"Grandmother told me you were working here. I thought you might like some company and maybe some help," he said without preamble.

As if sensing her confusion, he pulled open the screen door and walked in without waiting for an invitation. "So how about giving me a grand tour, and then you can tell me what you want me to do."

She stepped back almost automatically to allow him space. He was dressed in jeans again and a blue shirt that made his eyes look even bluer. She didn't remember the six-foot-square entry hall seeming so small before. "Harve, I don't think—"

"Hey, if you don't want me here, just say so, but I came to help. Really." The grin on his face was denied by the look in his eyes, as if he was uncertain of his welcome. "I can't claim to be a 'domestic engineer,' but my grandmother taught me the purpose of a broom along with my multiplication tables. Let me help you, Lottie."

"Somehow, I can't envision you doing..." She hesitated.

"What? Grunt labor?"

She nodded.

"I was twelve when my parents were killed in that boating accident on Beaver Lake and I went to live with my grandmother," he told her. "Abigail Tremayne is a firm believer in knowing how to do for yourself. I can wash clothes and dishes, make my own bed and wield a broom or a mop with the best of them. I'll admit I prefer to hire Annie to do my housekeeping, but that doesn't mean I couldn't do it if I had to. In an emergency I can even iron my own shirts. Come on, Lottie, give me a chance. I'm here. I'm willing. I work cheap. I also brought a thermos of coffee."

"How cheap?" she couldn't resist asking.

"Agree to have dinner with me tonight and we'll call it square."

"I don't know, Harve. Once I finish here, I'm not sure I'll have the energy to change for dinner."

"I'm not exactly dressed for the country club, either. We'll raid the refrigerator at the farm. Annie always leaves it stocked for the weekend. There. That's settled. Now show me what you've been doing."

Giving in to him was easier that arguing. Besides, she had to admit she'd like the company. *His* company, although exactly how much help he'd be remained to be seen.

"I've been concentrating in here and on one of the upstairs bedrooms," she told him as she led the way into the kitchen. "Then I can tackle the rest a little at a time."

Harve gave a low whistle as they entered the big country-style kitchen. He walked to the nearest cabinet and ran his hand over the wood. "Beautiful," he said. "Chestnut, isn't it? Did you refinish them?"

"Luckily they only needed a good cleaning. When I first saw the condition they were in, I was afraid I couldn't save them. They polished up nicely, though, didn't they?"

"Yes, they did. So what else are you doing?"

"The workmen are scheduled to lay the new floor tile next week. Then the appliances can be delivered. All I have left to do in here is strip the old paper off the wall and hang the new wallpaper I have on order. Then the kitchen will be finished. That's what I'm doing today—in the bedroom, I mean. Stripping wallpaper."

"You're kidding."

She gave him a puzzled look. "Believe me, stripping wallpaper is nothing to kid about."

"Lady, this is your lucky day," he said. "I told you I could wield a mop or broom and I can, but the truth is I haven't had much practice. Stripping wallpaper, however—now that's a different story.''

He hooked his thumbs in the waistband of his jeans, striking an exaggerated macho pose. "I am a wallpaper stripper extraordinaire. Did you know my grandmother completely repapers her house every three years, whether it needs it or not? She hasn't let me near a paste brush since I was fourteen and insisted on papering my own bedroom. I made a real botch of it. But stripping off the old paper was my job. That's a skill in which I can modestly claim to be an expert.''

She shook her head. "I don't know whether to believe you or not.''

"Believe me. Do you have sponges and a steamer?''

She nodded.

"Then lead the way and I'll prove it.''

He insisted on being the one to climb the ladder and loosen the paper at ceiling height. Six-foot-plus had a definite advantage when dealing with ten-foot ceilings, Lottie decided. They worked comfortably together and in only a short time had completed more than she could have hoped to accomplish in a full afternoon working by herself.

"Thank you, Harve,'' she told him when they stopped for a coffee break. "I would never have gotten so much done by myself.'' She settled herself on the floor and leaned back against the wall. He sat down beside her.

"We'll have the room finished in another hour," he said. "Ready to admit I am an expert?"

She grinned. "Without reservation. You are undoubtedly a wallpaper-stripping artiste." Then she added, "You make good coffee, too."

"Careful," he teased. "Such praise will give me a big head."

As they sat in compatible silence, sipping their coffee, her thoughts wandered back to what he'd told her about going to live with his grandmother. She looked at him. "Can I ask you a personal question?"

"Sure."

"When your parents died, were you angry?"

He set his coffee cup carefully on the floor and turned to face her. "Because they'd left me, you mean? Yes, I was. I think it's a normal part of the grieving process. I was lucky to have my grandmother. Outliving her own son had to be devastating, but she was always there for me. My parents had provided for me materially. She provided for me emotionally. She's an extraordinary lady. Still, I was angry for a long time."

"I was really angry with my father," Lottie said quietly. "I think I still am. Your parents' death was accidental. They had no choice. But my father chose to die. He made this incredible mess and then...just walked away, leaving my mother and me to deal with it."

She took a deep breath. "I lost my mother, too.

She didn't die, not then, but I lost her, anyway. She was so shattered and so bitter. At first I was mad at her, too. Why did she let my father kill himself? Daddy always did what she said. Why hadn't she stopped him? Then, well, she was so obviously a victim—I saw us both as victims—I got over being mad at her. Until I came back here and saw the house and then I think…I think I got mad at her all over again."

"Lottie…" His voice was gentle and she felt his arm go around her shoulders. Then he pulled her into his side. "Did you ever talk to anyone about this. An expert, I mean?"

She shook her head. "No. I think I discussed it in general terms with my psychology professor in college. You know, the mandatory psych 101 course, but nothing specific or personal."

"Well, I'm no expert, but I think what you felt, what you're feeling, is perfectly normal. You *are* a victim. So was your mother. Your father, too. I didn't know your father well—he was another generation. But from what I remember of him, he was a strong proud man. Dying as he did wouldn't have been a deliberate conscious decision. It was as much an accident as my parents' deaths."

"How can you say that? He deliberately drove his car off the top of a bluff into the lake."

"We're all human, Lottie. We make mistakes. How often, when you're under stress, when you're upset or angry, have you said something or done something only to regret it when you were feeling better? I think that's probably what happened to your father. I think that's probably what happens to most people who die the way your father did. The person makes an irrational decision, acting on the impulse of the moment—a decision he'll change as soon as he's thinking more clearly. Only sometimes—if the decision was a fatal one—he never gets that chance.''

"Do you really believe that?''

"Yes, I do—except for the unfortunate few who hear voices and the like. But you can't say that person's making a conscious decision, either. Life is too precious to waste, Lottie. Any rational person knows that, but a rational person can have irrational thoughts at times. Occasionally they end in tragedy. In my mind that qualifies as an accident.''

Lottie scrubbed at her damp eyes with a fist as he gave her shoulder a comforting squeeze.

"I wish you'd been around for me to talk to when my father died,'' she said in a wobbly voice.

"I don't know I would have been any help then,'' he told her. "Remember, I was young, healthy and, in my mind, indomitable. I'd locked the scars left by my parents' deaths in a closet marked No Trespassing. It took another death to prompt me to bring them out and examine them.''

"Your fiancée?''

He nodded. "Yes. Rosemary. She was so young and lovely and alive. Then she was gone. Just like that. I grieved for her for a long time. I think maybe I was grieving for my parents, too. Finally I was able to stop grieving and let the pain go. Then I was able to remember the good times.''

He paused. ''I honestly thought I'd dealt with it, but now I wonder if a person ever finishes dealing with that kind of loss. Oh, the immediate grief goes and eventually the pain, but you certainly never forget.'' He met her gaze. ''You know, Lottie, this is the first time I've ever tried putting all this into words. I think talking to you has been good for me.''

''I don't understand what you mean.''

He gave her shoulder another squeeze. ''I'm not sure I do, either. You know, Shakespeare once warned, 'What's gone and past help, should be past grief.' I think I sometimes forget that. Talking to you reminded me. Thank you, Lottie.''

She straightened under his arm. ''Why do you do that?''

''Do what?''

''Throw obscure quotations into your conversation.''

He laughed. ''I didn't realize I did it that often.''

''Take my word for it, you do.''

''And sound like a pontificating ass?'' He groaned.

''Well, maybe not that bad. A little pompous perhaps.'' She didn't even try to hide her grin.

''Vicki and I used to play a game,'' he said.

"We'd try to outdo each other in dredging up obscure quotations. So sometimes now I may unconsciously use a quotation because it conveys what I want to say better than I can myself. However, the next time you hear me sounding pompous you have my permission to call me on it."

He began to get to his feet. "Now, are you ready to go back to work? The sooner we're finished, the sooner we can eat."

They finished the room in what seemed to Lottie a very short time. Then, as promised, she followed Harve back to his farm for a quick evening meal. "I always seem to be thanking you," she told him as he walked her to her car afterward. "Thank you for the company and the expert labor and the dinner and...and our conversation."

"I was glad to help," he said. "I mean that, Lottie. I enjoyed it, too." He leaned forward and pressed a kiss to her forehead.

Like she was a little sister, she thought. Well, maybe that was best.

"When you're ready to strip more wallpaper, let me know," he said. "Okay?"

"Considering your expertise, that's an offer I won't refuse."

As she drove back to Abby's, she couldn't help thinking about her father and her mother—and her conversation with Harve. For the first time since her father's death, her anger toward him was fading. She'd never understand her father's reasoning or actions. Nor her mother's. Her father's decisions, planned or not, had set the rest of the tragedy in motion. But he'd escaped the consequences. She and her mother had lived with them for years.

Maybe Harve was right. Maybe all three of them were victims of circumstances beyond their control. What was past couldn't be changed. Maybe now she'd be able to accept, understand and then let go of her bitterness—toward both her father and her mother.

She had Harve to thank for that, she realized. It was the greatest gift he could have given her.

## CHAPTER EIGHT

As THE WEEK PROGRESSED, community support for the new banking hours continued to grow. An editorial in the biweekly *Gazette* praised the announcement, calling it a decision that "moves the Little Falls Bank into the 1990s and is a boon to the local business community and a convenience for area residents."

Lottie knew that an honest analysis of how much the expanded hours might help the bank wouldn't be available for several weeks, maybe not for months. The announcement was certainly a publicity bonanza, but she would have to wait to determine how many new customers it drew.

Fortunately Cyrus kept his displeasure confined to the inner chambers of the bank and out of the public eye. For once Lottie was grateful for his normal sour-looking countenance. To a casual observer he looked no grumpier than usual.

In addition to the community's goodwill, Lottie could see a bonus in the attitudes of the bank employees. It would have been pure stupidity to believe they hadn't realized that the bank was in financial trouble. Maybe they'd now begin to believe, or at least hope, they had a future.

Occasionally Lottie heard Jeff whistling under his breath in the next office. Josephine was smiling a lot more, even when she wasn't with a customer. Lottie thought she'd even seen the bookkeeper, sober-faced Hiram Nelson, crack an occasional smile. She could only hope they wouldn't be disappointed. But they, like she, would simply have to wait and see.

On Friday afternoon, convinced she'd done everything she could do in that department, Lottie returned her attention to the bank's investment portfolio. She'd already transferred available funds into higher-yield, but still conservative, insured treasury bonds. Later she hoped to reinvest some of the funds in more profitable higher-risk offerings, but the bank's reserves were too low to risk at the moment. She had to protect the depositors.

She'd left one block of funds in their original bond investment account after Cyrus had furnished her with the information on early-withdrawal penalties. The bonds were scheduled to mature in three months. If she pulled them before maturity, the bank would pay more in penalties than they would make in increased interest for the same period.

She now turned her attention to that account. It was the same account that had intrigued her the previous week. As she slowly scrolled through the records, she was again unable to shake the feeling she was missing something.

Yes, the return was low, but then, Cyrus always invested cautiously. The earnings were meticulously posted and seemed consistent. The totals balanced. She followed the pattern back through the previous year, becoming more puzzled and more concerned.

What was she seeing? What was she *not* seeing? When interest rates were as low as these, bank funds were normally invested in short-term bonds to allow the bank to take advantage of higher interest rates when they became available. Yet nothing had changed in this account for more than a year.

How much further back did the pattern go? The bank had put its accounts on-line only a couple of years ago. She'd need to examine the records in the basement vault to determine if the same pattern was in place before the conversion. At any rate, she could do nothing more today.

The last hour was as slow as usual for a mid-month banking day. Mildred Gaston stopped by to deposit the small insurance check she received each month. Lottie suggested she have the check electronically deposited. "It's quicker, more efficient, and you don't risk it being lost or going astray in the mails," she explained.

But like many of the town's older residents, Mildred resisted such "newfangled" ideas. "It's not that I don't trust the bank," she told Lottie, "but I like to hold the check in my hand. That way, I know I really have it."

Just before closing time, Jacob Calley brought in his morning receipts for deposit. Calley was one local businessman who'd enthusiastically endorsed the new Saturday hours. He looked around as if to see if anyone could overhear, then leaned across the counter. "Friday nights and Saturday mornings are my busiest times," he said in a whisper. "I don't like leaving that kind of money lying around the store over the weekend, so I've been hauling it home. Figure that's not too safe, either, but it was the best I could do. You'll sure enough see me every Saturday morning right before noon, and I can tell you, that'll be a load off my mind. So thank you kindly, little lady. If anyone asks me, you got my vote."

"Thank *you*, Mr. Calley," she said, "and thank you for your loyalty to the bank."

"That goes both ways," he said in his usual gruff voice. "Little Falls is lucky to have the bank. Sure don't like to think about having to drive all the way down to Fayetteville or over to Springdale to do my business. Don't know how long the town'd last like that. Leastways, it wouldn't be the same. That's for sure."

And that, Lottie thought, was exactly why the bank was as important to the town as the town was to the bank. The two had existed in a symbiotic relationship since the beginning.

Lottie tallied and cleared the teller's drawer, then logged off her computer for the day. On impulse she decided to stop in at the Down Home before heading to her house to work for a few hours. A dose of Myrtle was always good for the soul.

"Hey, Lottie," Myrtle called as Lottie stepped inside the almost deserted café. "Grab yourself a table and I'll join you. Be good to get out from behind this counter for a minute. What'll you have?"

Lottie sat down at one of the tables. "Just a cup of coffee. I only stopped by to say hello."

"And about time I'd say." Myrtle handed her a steaming mug of coffee, set a second cup down on the opposite side of the table and then sat in front of it. "You ready to tell me what's going on between you and Harve Tremayne?"

"Going on?" Lottie nearly choked on her coffee. Carefully she lowered her cup down and tried to catch her breath. "Whatever gave you the idea there was anything going on between Harve and me?"

"Well, now, the way I heard it, you and him went horseback riding over at his farm early Saturday morning. That right?"

"Yes, but—" she started.

"Then I heard the two of you were alone all Sunday afternoon in that empty house of yours.

And *then* I heard you went back to his farm with him and were there together until after dark,'' she finished on a note of triumph. ''Now that sounds to me like something's going on.''

*Oh, heavens, I should have remembered,* Lottie thought. *Nothing escapes notice in Little Falls, and all stories lead to the Down Home.* She forced herself to stay calm. ''There is absolutely nothing going on between Harve and me,'' she said firmly. ''We're just friends.''

''Well, now, I'm sorry to hear that.'' Myrtle shook her head. ''He's a right handsome fellow. The two of you make a fine-looking couple. You sure there's nothing going on? Seems to me I remember you were sweet on him once upon a time.''

Lottie felt the heat rise in her cheeks and ducked her head. In addition to being one of the town's most flamboyant characters, Myrtle was also one of its most perceptive. ''That was nothing but a teenage crush,'' she protested. ''Harve was helping me strip wallpaper Sunday. Then I followed him back to the farm and we raided the refrigerator for dinner. We're just friends,'' she repeated.

''If you say so. Still, it seems a shame.'' There was regret in Myrtle's voice. ''Been worried about that boy for the last few years. Once he stopped grieving for that fiancée of his, I thought everything would be all right. But it's not. He's just walking through life. Not especially sad, but not exactly happy, either. You'd be good for him. Shake him up some. Still, I guess if he don't ring your bells, then he don't ring your bells."

"Ring my bells?"

"Well, that's what it's all about, you know—the birds and the bees and everything. You're right to hold out for that kind of feeling. Take me and my Chester now. Knew the first time I saw him that he was the man for me. Not that I was ready to admit it. I mean, I ask you, why would any girl want to move halfway across the country to a hick town so tiny it didn't even have a movie house? Still, Chester won in the end.

"So you hold out for that kind of feeling. You'll know when it happens. You'll look at him and your insides'll kinda jiggle."

"Sounds uncomfortable," Lottie said, wishing Myrtle would change the subject.

Myrtle, however, was not about to. "Sometimes it is," she said, and gave Lottie a piercing look from under her mascara-ladened eyelashes. "Especially if you're trying to pretend it didn't happen. It's also the most glorious feeling in the world. You'll know it's happening when you're thinking about something else, something completely different, and then, suddenly there he'll be—in your head. I tell you, girl, that's when you might as well give in and admit that he's the one."

The conversation was hitting a little too close to home for Lottie. "I still say, it doesn't sound very comfortable, but in this case, it doesn't matter.

Harve and I are just friends,'' she insisted once again.

Lottie was saved from further discussion of the subject when the bell above the café door jingled. ''Well, now, guess that's the end of my break,'' Myrtle said, rising from the table and moving back behind the counter.

Lottie breathed a sigh of relief and quickly finished her cup of coffee, then, while Myrtle was still busy, waved a cheery goodbye and slipped out of the café.

It didn't matter how jiggly her insides were, she told herself firmly. It was as clear as the moon on a cloudless night that any feelings Harve held for her were strictly those of friendship.

HARVE TOLD HIMSELF he and Lottie were just friends. He told himself he'd offered her his help only because of shared childhood memories and the long-standing friendship between their two families. That was what friends were for.

So what was he doing thinking about her?

She could be prickly as a cactus pear or as tender as a newborn foal, as vulnerable as a declawed kitten or as infuriating as a burr under a saddle.

She rebuffed his offers of assistance and ignored his suggestions. She frustrated and soothed him. She charmed and challenged him.

She certainly never bored him.

Dammit, she was tying him in knots.

Uncomfortable with the direction of his thoughts, he pushed his chair away from his desk, picked up his coffee cup and strolled toward the kitchen, meeting his housekeeper on the way.

"I was just coming to tell you I'm about ready to leave," Annie said. "I put a casserole in the refrigerator for tomorrow. There's another one in the freezer. All you have to do is heat them up in the microwave. You need me to do anything else before I go?"

"No, thank you, Annie. I'll be fine," he told her.

"You're sure? I've got time to whip up a quick pie—if you think you might be having company."

"Not that I know of."

"Oh. All right, but I thought I'd ask just in case."

He set the coffee cup down and propped himself against the counter. "Just in case? Okay, Annie. Why don't you tell me what you're getting at, instead of just hinting?"

She stuck out her chin. "Well, I thought you might be having Miss Lottie over for dinner again. I wanted everything to be nice."

"And where did you hear Miss Lottie had been here for dinner?" he asked softly.

"Wasn't she? Everybody says—" Annie broke off abruptly.

"Everybody says what?"

"Everybody says she was here for supper last Sunday night," she admitted defiantly. "If you'd told me she was coming, Mr. Harve, I could've fixed you something extra nice. That's why I wanted to know if she was coming again this weekend. I don't want you feeding her leftovers twice in a row. She'll think I don't take good care of you."

"Did Lottie complain that I'd fed her leftovers?"

Annie snorted. "Of course not. She'd never do anything like that. Even as a little girl, Lottie was the most appreciative child I've ever seen. I could have fed her peanut-butter sandwiches on stale bread and she'd thank me just like I'd given her a four-star meal. Not that I ever did of course."

Usually Annie was plain-speaking. This time, however, he was having trouble following her. "Never did what?"

"Gave her sandwiches on stale bread of course. You should know better than that. Have I ever fed you stale bread?" Her expression was as indignant as a cat caught in a rainstorm.

He allowed himself a grin. "No, of course not. You always serve excellent meals, Annie. I didn't mean to imply you didn't. I simply lost the track of the conversation for a moment."

"Well, pay attention. Now, are you sure she won't be coming over again this weekend? I've got some fresh blackberries in the refrigerator. The Clayton boys came by selling them."

"Fresh berries? Already?"

"We've had such nice spring weather this year they're in early," she told him. "Nothing better than fresh blackberry pie and ice cream. It always was one of Miss Lottie's favorites.''

It suddenly occurred to Harve that he might be missing an opportunity. Although he'd known Lottie as a playmate, she was closer in age to his cousin Vicki and so had been more Vicki's friend than his. As the Carlyle housekeeper, Annie had probably known Lottie, the child, better than anyone.

"To tell you the truth, Annie, last Sunday night was a spur-of-the-moment thing. We don't have any plans for this weekend. However, that's not to say it might not happen again,'' he added thoughtfully. "Especially if I had one of your blackberry pies as a bribe.''

"Well, then, why don't I just whip one up before I leave?''

It was easy to detect the approval in her voice. He smiled. "I'd appreciate it, if you're sure you have time?''

"Doesn't take any time to build a pie,'' she assured him. "I'll set the timer and when it buzzes, all you have to do is take it out of the oven.''

"If it won't distract you while you're working, I'll keep you company,'' he said, carefully keeping the satisfaction out of his voice. Annie loved to talk, but if she figured out he wanted to pump her, she might not. He poured himself a cup of coffee and pulled a stool to the counter.

"Won't bother me none at all, Mr. Harve.''

He watched for a moment or two as she bustled

around collecting ingredients and utensils. She turned on the oven, then retrieved a bowl of blackberries from the refrigerator and set them on the counter behind her.

"Have you had a chance to visit with Lottie much since she's been back?" he asked.

"She's come by to see me a couple of times," Annie told him as she measured a couple of cups of flour into a mixing bowl. "Lottie knows I like to see her. She always was a thoughtful child."

"Do you think she's changed much? Since she was a child, I mean."

"Some, maybe. Growing up'll do that to you. I think she's more cautious now. Not as quick to throw her heart over the rainbow, then chase after it, so to speak. She had a rough time after she and her mother left Little Falls. It was bound to change her."

Annie added shortening and water to the bowl, combining the mixture with deft fingers. Harve watched, intrigued, as she sprinkled flour on the counter, then twisted off a blob of dough from the bowl, placed it in the middle of the flour-covered counter and began wielding the wooden rolling pin like a gourmet pastry chef.

"Anyway, Lottie's still the same little girl I knew—sweet, loyal and optimistic. She still gives her best and she doesn't understand others when they don't."

Satisfied finally with the thickness of the dough,

Annie lifted it from the counter and draped it over a pie plate. She sprinkled the countertop with flour again, pinched another piece of dough from the bowl and repeated the rolling process.

"May as well make two pies while I'm at it," she explained. Then she went on, "When Lottie first got back here, I heard some talk that maybe she'd come home to get even with her uncle or maybe the town," Annie said darkly, "but I didn't believe it for a minute. That girl doesn't have a mean bone in her body."

Annie draped the rolled dough over a second pie plate, then reached for the bowl of berries on the counter behind her.

"Ah, these are sweet," she said, after popping one into her mouth. She pushed the bowl toward him. "Here, try one."

The taste of blackberry *was* sweet, but there was also an unexpected tartness. Like Lottie, Harve thought.

"You know, Lottie didn't need to come back here," Annie said as if in afterthought. "I bet one of the bigger banks would be happy to buy her out."

Annie retrieved a lemon from the refrigerator, cut it in half with a quick slice of her knife, squeezed the juice into a cup and set it aside. "Come to think of it, she'd probably make more money selling it than trying to save it. I ask you now, would she be working so hard at the bank and trying to fix up that old house of hers if she was planning to sell?''

"I agree with you, Annie," Harve said. "I think she came back here because she wants to save the bank. And because she wants to live here." *At least, that's what I want to believe,* he thought.

Annie opened the jar of molasses she'd set on the counter earlier and measured a bit of the thick brown syrup into the berries, then added the lemon juice and part of a cup of sugar. She stirred the mixture together and sampled the concoction.

"Well, now," she said, "that's better." He wasn't sure if she was referring to the pie filling or to his comment on Lottie's intentions. "Still, needs a little something, though. Hand me the nutmeg and cinnamon from the spice rack behind you, Mr. Harve," she ordered.

Annie took the two spice containers from him, sprinkled a little from each into the berry mixture, then stirred again. "I tell you one thing," she continued without looking up. "Lottie has learned to hide her feelings. When she was a little girl, you could tell what she was thinking just by looking at her. It's not so easy now." Annie sighed. "But I guess she had to learn how just for her own protection. Like I said before, she hasn't had an easy time of it."

Annie gave the berries another stir and sampled again. "Well, now, I'd say that's just about perfect." She divided the berry mixture, pouring half into each pie shell, then took the last of the pastry mixture and begin rolling it out.

"The secret of a good berry pie is to release the sweetness of the berries without disguising or diluting it," she added. "Sometimes it takes a little something extra, a little something unexpected, to do that."

"Like the cinnamon and nutmeg?" he asked.

"Yes," she said. "They're unexpected." She put several dollops of butter on top of the berries, then cut the remaining crust dough, now rolled thin, into strips and began weaving a lattice on the tops of the pies. After removing the excess dough from around the pie plates with a sharp knife, she used the prongs of a fork to crimp the top and bottom edges of the crust together. "There. All done but the baking," she announced.

She slipped the pies into the oven. "You listen for the timer, Mr. Harve," she instructed. "I've set it for thirty minutes. It might take a little longer. Check them when the buzzer goes off, then about every five minutes. Be sure to let them cool before you put them in the refrigerator."

"I can handle that," he assured her. He sniffed the air appreciatively. "You can already smell them. They're going to be delicious."

"No reason they shouldn't be," she said. "Comes from having good ingredients to start with."

He grinned. "Thank you for staying to make

them," he told her. "I'll clean up. I've kept you here long enough."

"You're sure?"

"I'm positive. You get along. Have a good weekend."

"Well, if you're sure...I'll just get my purse."

Annie returned to the kitchen a moment later, stopped by the back door and gave him a piercing look. "I've got one more thing to say about Miss Lottie," she announced. "You're a plumb fool if you let her get away."

"Annie—"

"And don't forget, sometimes it takes a little something unexpected to release the sweetness." With that she disappeared out the door.

Harve managed to control his laughter until Annie disappeared from sight. Just who'd been pumping whom in that encounter? Apparently his housekeeper knew him as well, if not better, than he knew himself.

It didn't matter. He sniffed the air appreciatively again. After all, he'd gotten two blackberry pies out of the experience, hadn't he?

## CHAPTER NINE

AFTER LEAVING the Down Home, Lottie drove to her house, changed into the set of work clothes she'd stored there and began stripping wallpaper in the kitchen. The new wallpaper was the last job to be done before her new appliances were delivered.

In spite of best intentions, she couldn't help wishing Harve was there to help. Not only the work, but time seemed to move faster when he was around.

On second thought, maybe it was just as well he wasn't. There was enough gossip about them already.

She worked steadily until just before dark, then put her tools away and looked around, satisfied with the way the restoration was progressing. The new kitchen floor had been laid on schedule, and she hoped to hang the new wallpaper this weekend.

The lingering twilight had faded to darkness by the time she left her house to drive to Abby's. After the hustle and bustle of Saint Louis, she found herself enjoying the peace and quiet of Little Falls. Tonight her car was the only vehicle on the farm-to-market road in the sparsely settled countryside.

She was humming along with an old Beatles tune on the radio when she entered one particularly lonely stretch of road and felt the steering wheel jerk under her hands.

Damn! It had been a while since she'd heard that ominous thumping sound, but there was no forgetting it—a flat. She muttered an unladylike expression and eased the car to the side of the road.

Her father had taught her to change a tire at the same time he'd taught her to drive, but it was one skill she hadn't used often in Saint Louis.

Still muttering, she retrieved a flashlight from the glove compartment and got out of the car to survey the damage. Within minutes she'd collected the necessary equipment from the trunk, pulled the spare tire from its holding rack and assembled the jack under the car frame near the right rear wheel.

She propped the flashlight in the dirt, then, carefully following the routine her father had taught her years ago, began to remove the lug nuts. "One from the bottom, one from the top, one from the left, one from the right," she chanted to herself as she laid the nuts inside the overturned hubcap so they wouldn't be accidentally lost in the dirt. Amazing how quickly the almost forgotten instructions came back to her.

Her Waterloo was the sixth and final lug nut. No matter what she tried—coaxing, swearing, kicking, even jumping on the arm of the lug wrench—nothing worked. The nut refused to budge.

Panting, she slumped against the side of the car and considered her options. She could wait and hope for assistance from a passing motorist—assuming one happened along—or she could begin the hike to Abby's.

Since the chances of a motorist driving by on this road at this time of night hovered somewhere between zilch and zero, she had little choice. She'd have to hike.

She'd only been walking about ten minutes when she saw the headlights of an approaching vehicle. City-learned survival skills made her consider ducking out of sight, but then she realized it was probably too late. In the darkness of the country road, the flashlight beam would have been clearly visible. Besides, this was Little Falls, not Saint Louis. Even if she didn't know the approaching motorist, area residents were more likely to offer assistance than harm.

Still, it was with a slight feeling of apprehension that she stepped to the side of the road and watched the headlights come closer.

It was a truck, and as it pulled off the road, its headlights caught her in their glare. Unable to see anything, she took a firm grip on the flashlight and backed up a step.

"Is that you, Lottie?"

Her knees nearly buckled in relief when she recognized Harve's voice. "Yes, it's me," she answered as he stepped in front of the headlights and walked toward her.

"What the devil are you doing out on the road at this time of night?" His voice was gruff and demanding.

"Oh, just taking an evening stroll," she said sweetly. Then her tone changed. "Honestly, Harve, do you think I'm out here just for the fun of it?"

He stopped in front of her. With the glare of the headlights behind him, she couldn't see his expression, but his body language was easy enough to read.

"Okay, I'm sorry," he said, his voice not exactly contrite. "It's only that I...you scared me when I saw you walking by yourself."

"I'll admit to being a little scared myself. I'm glad to see you."

"What's wrong? Car trouble?"

"Flat tire. And before you ask, yes, I do know how to change a tire. But one of the lug nuts seems frozen."

"I don't suppose you have a cell phone. Then you could've called for help," he said.

"No. I don't have a cell phone. What are you doing out here, anyway?"

"Looking for you. Grandmother was worried when it got dark and you weren't home."

"Oh, no." Although Abby was careful not to interfere in her affairs, Lottie knew her hostess kept a discreet eye on her comings and goings. So of course she'd become concerned when Lottie failed to arrive home after dark. "I'm sorry I worried her," she told him.

"Which is why I'll get you a phone tomorrow. You shouldn't be out here alone at night."

"I can get my own phone." Lottie sighed in exasperation. "Darn it, Harve, you're acting like I had a flat tire on purpose. Besides, this is Little Falls, not Saint Louis. I would've been perfectly all right."

"Meanness isn't confined to the big city, Lottie."

"I know that, but no one except locals use this road, especially at this time of night. I haven't seen a soul except you, and you came looking for me. If we weren't standing here talking, I'd be nearly home by now."

"Lottie." His voice held a distinct note of warning.

"Oh, all right. I'll order a cell phone tomorrow. Satisfied?"

"I will be when I see the phone."

Under her breath Lottie slowly counted from one to ten.

"Come on," Harve said. "I'll call grandmother from the truck and then we'll see if I can help with the tire."

*He*, of course, would have a cell phone, Lottie thought, then immediately felt contrite. He was only trying to help. He was probably right about getting a cell phone, too, if for no other reason than peace of mind.

But he wasn't *always* right. She doubted if he'd be able to break that lug nut loose.

"That nut's stuck tight," she said.

"I'm not doubting your word, Lottie, but I do have a slight weight advantage," he said. "If I can't break it loose, we'll let Clyde at the service station handle it."

As they drove down the road to her car, he called Abby to tell her Lottie had a flat tire but was fine.

He was, as Lottie had predicted, no more successful with the lug nut than she'd been. Finally admitting defeat, he turned the truck around and headed toward his grandmother's.

"Aren't you going to take me to Clyde's? I have to go to work tomorrow," she protested when she realized what he was doing.

"I'll take care of it," he told her in his don't-argue voice, "and I'll pick you up in the morning. What time do you need to be at the bank? Nine?"

Knowing it was be useless to protest, she nodded mutely. The sooner she could move into her own house, the better off she'd be, she told herself again. Then, even if she had car trouble, she'd be able to walk to the bank.

They rode in silence the rest of the way. When he pulled in the back of his grandmother's house, he cut the engine and was out of the truck before she had time to protest.

"Give me your car keys and I'll take them to Clyde," he said as he walked with her to the door. "I'm sure he'll have you back on the road when you get off work tomorrow. I'll pick you up at eight-forty-five in the morning. That should give us time to get you to town."

Lottie nodded and handed him the keys. "Harve, I'm...well, thank you for coming to my rescue. I might not have sounded grateful, but I am."

"I know that," he said, "and I didn't mean to act like an ogre. I was worried about you."

"I...I'm sorry."

"It's all right." He hesitated, then raised his hand and brushed her cheek with his fingers. "Get a good night's sleep. I'll see you in the morning."

And that was that, she thought, ignoring the hammering of her heart.

LOTTIE WORE her red suit the next morning, sort of in celebration of the bank's first Saturday opening, which to her mind qualified as a red-letter day. Besides, the suit made her feel good—feminine, yet professional.

Determined to be no more of a nuisance than necessary, she was ready when Harve arrived, this time in a late-model sedan, instead of his truck. He gave a low appreciative whistle. "I like you in red," he said.

Flustered, Lottie managed to stammer a thank-you. "Where's the truck?" she asked, more for something to say than out of genuine curiosity.

"I thought we'd be more comfortable in the car," he told her. "Clyde towed yours in last night. He should have it ready for you when the bank closes. I'll pick you up at noon and drive you to the garage, then we'll see about getting you a phone."

She should have known. Once Harve got an idea in his head, he was like a dog with a bone. Still, it was too beautiful a day to let his high-handed manner destroy her mood.

"All right," she agreed meekly.

He shot her a suspicious look. "What are you planning now, Lottie Carlyle?" he demanded.

"I plan to work until noon, then pick up my car at Clyde's and then go buy a car phone," she told him, "Exactly as you ordered."

"Lottie…"

"What's wrong, Harve? Isn't that what you told me to do?"

"All right, all right. I did sound a little bossy and I have no right to order you around. But dammit, Lottie, it's for your own good."

"I know that," she said. "That's why I agreed, even if you do remind me of a general directing his troops. Can I buy a cell phone in town, or will I need to go to Springdale?"

"We'll find a better selection in Fayetteville," he said.

She cleared her throat.

"I mean, *you'll* probably find more of a choice in Fayetteville," he corrected himself. "I'd be happy to come with you," he added. "In fact, I've got an errand I need to run down there, anyway."

"That's why you brought the car, isn't it?" she said with sudden understanding.

"It's more comfortable for a trip to the city," he admitted. "I intended..." He cleared his throat. "I hoped you'd let me come with you. As I said, I have an errand to run. I also know the best stores. That is, if you'd like my assistance."

Lottie turned her head so he wouldn't see her grin. "In that case, I'd welcome your company. Now see? That wasn't so hard, was it?"

She accepted his grunt as an affirmative and grinned again.

The bank stayed busy during its first Saturday opening hours. Many customers were downtown businessmen, but she also saw several unfamiliar faces. She personally opened two new accounts and several times during the morning saw Jeff with people she hoped were also new customers.

One young man introduced himself as Samuel Morgan and scheduled an appointment for late Monday afternoon, following his classes at the university in Fayetteville. She told him if he didn't make it to the bank by three, she'd wait until he arrived.

Even before the bank closed she was ready to

declare the Saturday hours a success. She wouldn't be able to determine exactly how successful until after closing, but it looked good.

Harve arrived only minutes before noon. Lottie put him in her office to wait, then after the bank doors were locked, helped Josephine tally her drawer.

Jeff was all smiles. "I opened three new accounts," he told them. "Two were old customers who said they were glad we'd decided to open Saturdays, but one was a brand-new customer."

"I had one returnee and one new one, too," Lottie said, her grin as wide as his. "That's five new accounts. We can't expect to do as well every Saturday, but it's a great start."

Leaving Jeff to lock the cash in the vault, Lottie carried the paperwork to her office and set it in her basket to file on Monday.

Her mood must have been apparent.

"A good day?" Harve asked.

"Five new accounts," she told him. "Yes, I think we can say it's been a very good day."

Clyde was waiting for them when they arrived at the service station. "You had a puncture through the sidewall," he told her.

Lottie frowned. "I thought I'd run over a nail or a piece of wire."

"No, it was a sidewall puncture," he repeated. "Don't worry, though. It was an easy patch. Fixed it good as new."

"But what caused it?"

He shrugged. "No way of telling. It happens."

"Did you have any trouble getting that wheel off?" Harve asked him. "I couldn't get it to budge."

"It was a real bitch." Clyde's face went scarlet. "Pardon me, Ms. Carlyle," he said, ducking his head, "I mean, it was a real devil of a job getting that lug nut off."

He shifted his weight from one foot to the other, then raised his head. "Can I ask you a question, Ms. Carlyle?"

"Of course."

"Who changed that wheel last?"

She thought for a moment. "The service garage I used in Saint Louis. Yes, that's right. They switched my mud and snow tires and balanced and rotated the wheels in March."

"And you never took your hubcap off?"

"Not until last night when I tried to change the tire. Why?"

"Because the son of a...the guy who put on that wheel shouldn't be allowed around a car. At first I thought someone had just cross-threaded the nut when they screwed it on. That's an accident that can happen to anyone, but I tell you, Ms. Carlyle, I've never seen a bolt as mangled as that one."

Harve straightened. "What are you saying?" he asked Clyde.

"That bolt was hit with something hard, smash-

ing the threads after the nut was on. Pure carelessness. No way anyone could have screwed that lug
nut off. I had to cut it off.

"Now, don't you worry none, Ms. Carlyle," he
said, turning back to Lottie. "I rethreaded the bolt
for you. It's fixed all right and tight now, but if I
were you, I sure wouldn't take my car back to that
garage. Nobody needs that kind of aggravation."

"Thanks for the advice," she told him, "but I
don't expect to be using them again. You'll be getting my business now. That is, if you want it…"

He grinned. "I'll do a real good job for you, Ms.
Carlyle. If it's something I can't handle, I'll tell you
right up front. You can call on me anytime."

"You made Clyde's day," Harve told her as they
walked across the lot to her car. "He's a good me-
chanic. He knows his way around an engine."

"If I want the residents of Little Falls to patronize our bank, I need to return the favor," she said.
"Besides, I remember Clyde Ashton. I think his
uncle took care of my first car, but Clyde was already working at the garage. I figure if he's running
the garage now, he must know what he's doing.
Even if it is the only place in town, the local residents wouldn't patronize him if he didn't."

"When did you get so smart?" he asked.

"I've always been smart," she replied. "You
simply didn't notice."

"I have to confess, you grew up when I wasn't
looking," he said thoughtfully.

"I wasn't around."

"Well, you are now," he said, "and I'll warn you, Lottie Carlyle, I sometimes make mistakes, but I rarely make the same one twice."

Now what, she wondered, did he mean by that?

HARVE HAD A FROWN on his face as he watched Lottie pull out of the station. He'd told her he'd pick her up at her house for their trip to Fayetteville as soon as he filled the gas tank. He didn't need gas. What he needed were answers.

As soon as she disappeared from sight, he spun on his heel and marched back into Clyde's office. "Could it have been deliberate?" he asked without preamble.

"Deliberate? What?" Clyde asked, puzzled.

"Any of it. The flat tire? The mangled bolt? Either? Both?"

"I suppose," Clyde said after a moment. "But that don't make any sense, Mr. Tremayne. Why would anyone deliberately puncture a tire? Or mangle a bolt?"

"That's exactly what I'm wondering, but the coincidence of both happening at the same time bothers me. You said the bolt was damaged after the lug nut was on," he persisted.

"Well, sure, Mr. Tremayne. Otherwise no one could have screwed the nut on."

"But how could something like that happen? I mean accidentally?"

Clyde frowned. "I don't know. Maybe someone knocked against it with a lug wrench. Like I said earlier, pure carelessness."

Harve thought for a moment. "Can you estimate how long ago it happened? I mean, was the bolt clean?"

"It was clean, but that don't mean nothing. Ms. Carlyle said she hadn't taken off the hubcap."

"So it could have happened last March when she had her tires rotated. Or it could have happened yesterday?"

The expression on Clyde's face grew more perplexed. "I guess so."

"And the flat itself. You said the break was in the sidewall?"

Clyde nodded. "Small puncture. About half an inch from the rim. It would've taken several hours for the wheel to go flat."

"Any idea what might have caused it? I mean specifically."

Clyde scratched his head with one grimy finger. "Scraping up against a nail or a piece of wire maybe."

"Scraping? Was the sidewall scuffed?"

"Well, no," Clyde said. "It looked like a straight-in puncture. Why are you asking all these questions, Mr. Tremayne?"

"I'm just trying to figure out how she could have accidentally punctured the sidewall," he said, "especially when most of the time she only drives the highway from town to my grandmother's house.''

"But I hear she's fixing up her old house here in town," Clyde said. "There's always things like that around construction work."

"That's true," Harve agreed. "Could you estimate the size of whatever it was that caused the puncture? Could it have been something like a piece of chicken wire?"

"Nope, not substantial enough. It would have to've been a heavier-gauge wire—about as thick as, say, a penny nail."

"Or an ice pick?" Harve asked softly.

"Well, yeah, an ice pick could have done it, but that would mean— Lordy, Mr. Tremayne, you don't think someone did it deliberately, do you?"

"I don't know. I hope not, but the whole thing seems a little strange. Maybe I've just got a suspicious mind. Listen, Clyde, let's keep this conversation between the two of us. No need worrying Ms. Carlyle unnecessarily."

"Okay, if you say so, Mr. Tremayne." Clyde frowned. "But if someone did it on purpose...well, I mean, that kind of mischief, she could've been hurt. Someone ought to keep a close eye out for her."

"I intend to do just that," Harve assured him.

Was he imagining things? Being overly suspicious? Could Lottie's flat tire and the mangled lug bolt really be coincidence, or was something sinister going on?

He picked Lottie up at her house, and as they drove to Fayetteville, he glanced over at her. She appeared to have accepted Clyde's explanation that "things happen" without question. Surely, if she had any idea the incident was deliberate, she'd show some sign of it. But she looked cheerful. And relaxed. And beautiful.

Maybe he was overreacting.

He swallowed a sigh and stole another look. He hadn't been just flattering her earlier this morning when he told her he liked her in red. The truth was he liked her in anything, even the tattered jeans and faded shirt she'd worn when they worked at her house last Sunday.

She wasn't beauty-queen pretty, he decided. No, Lottie's was more of a quiet beauty. It was evident in the arrangement of her features, her generous mouth, flashing green eyes and dark hair—a beauty born in the genes, imbedded in the bone structure and enhanced, not by makeup, but by the spirit that shone from within. She would age gracefully, would still be attractive at ninety.

Would she still be invading his thoughts, breaking his concentration, disturbing his peace of mind then?

Probably, he conceded.

He smiled and Lottie was quick to notice. "What's so funny?" she asked.

"Nothing important," he said. "I'm hungry. I know a little place that serves the best barbecue north of the Pecos. Why don't we stop there for lunch before looking for your phone?"

"I was hoping to get back to Little Falls in time to do some work at the house this afternoon."

"It won't take long and it's on the way. Besides, you have to eat sometime. It might as well be now. After we eat, we'll find you a phone and be on our way back home in no time."

"I thought you had an errand to run, too."

"I…uh… Mine won't take more than a minute," he lied. What had he been thinking? She'd caught him completely off guard. Under normal circumstances he could bluff his way out of a boardroom of sharks. It wouldn't work with Lottie. She was the only person he knew who affected him this way. He felt a flush creep up his neck.

"You don't have an errand, do you?" It was more a statement than a question. "You said you did. I wouldn't have agreed to come with you otherwise."

"I do have an errand," he all but growled.

"Okay, what is it?"

"To get you a phone."

"Harve—" her indignation turned her eyes emerald green "—of all the conniving… I told you I'd get a phone. I don't need you to hold my hand."

"Ah, come on, Lottie. Don't be mad," he pleaded. "I like holding your hand, figuratively speaking of course. I know you said you'd get a phone and I believe you. But it is my errand in a way. After all, it's for my grandmother's peace of mind. And mine. Is it a crime to want to come with you? Haven't you figured out yet that I enjoy being with you?''

She still didn't relent. "Oh…you… Sometimes you make me so mad I could spit nails.''

"Whew, you had me worried there for a minute, short stuff. I thought you were really mad.''

"Darn it, Harve. Don't call me short stuff.''

"Pax, Lottie,'' he said, laughing. "Now can we go eat?''

After filling themselves with barbecued ribs and baked beans, which Lottie admitted were some of the best she'd ever eaten, Harve drove to an electronics store in the mall. He asked to see a deluxe-model cell phone. She insisted on examining an economy version.

He pulled her discreetly to the side. "Look, Lottie, I can advance you—''

She turned on him. "I don't need your money any more than I need that phone with all the bells and whistles,'' she said. "All I want is something to carry in the car in case I get stranded again. Okay?''

He retreated a step and threw up his hands. "I've made you mad again. I didn't mean to. I only wanted you to have the best phone. I'm sorry, Lottie.''

She sighed. "No, I'm the one who's sorry. I overreacted. At least, you didn't offer to buy it for me."

"Sometimes I'm dense, but I'm not dumb," he said. "Friends?"

"Friends," she agreed.

"Then buy your phone and let's get out of here."

# CHAPTER TEN

HOW DID HARVE do it? Lottie wondered. And why did she let him?

She'd been determined to say goodbye to him as soon as they returned to Little Falls. Yet here she was, still with him. After working together at the house for most of the afternoon, she now found herself on the way out to Tremayne Farm to raid the refrigerator. Again.

When they returned from Fayetteville, he'd told her to drive to Abby's where he would pick her up for the ride back to town. "No need taking two vehicles," he said.

He'd dismissed her worries about gossip. "You know Little Falls, Lottie," he told her. "There's always talk. It'll disappear as soon as something more interesting happens."

She realized she'd given in with only token resistance, knew she'd capitulated so easily because she liked being with him. Besides, she'd also known that with his help she'd be able to accomplish more than if she was working by herself.

*That's taking advantage. Shame on you,* her conscience scolded.

*Maybe, but he wanted to do it,* her practical mind had argued back.

She'd remained adamant about one thing. She wasn't going to have dinner at the farm. She was convinced that was what had started all the talk.

"Nonsense," he'd argued. "You're in no danger of becoming Little Falls's scarlet lady."

Then he'd bribed her. With a blackberry pie.

"How did you know I couldn't resist one of Annie's berry pies?" she asked.

"I told Annie I might need an incentive," Harve confessed.

"Well, it worked," Lottie said. *Annie Martin has a lot to answer for. No, that isn't fair,* she admitted. *I'm here because I want to be.*

Once she'd come to terms with her own culpability, she relaxed and decided to enjoy herself.

After eating, Harve suggested a dip in the hot tub. "Vicki always leaves a suit here for when she and her husband visit from Washington. You can borrow it. I don't know about you, but I used muscles today I'd forgotten I had."

This time she didn't even try to convince herself she shouldn't. A relaxing dip in the hot tub sounded like the perfect end to her day.

She changed into the swimsuit, then joined Harve in a gazebo located a few feet from the back porch. "Good heavens, this looks more like a swimming pool than a hot tub," she told him. "What do you do? Use it as a therapy pool for your horses?"

"They have their own. I also have a swimming pool, but I drain it in the winter. I haven't refilled it yet this spring." He shrugged. "What can I say? I'm a big man. I like room to move around."

"Well, I for one, will be content to simply sit and soak."

Lottie slipped into the clear water, perched for a moment on one of the built-in seats, then shifted to a lower one and with a sigh of bliss, immersed herself to her neck. Leaning her head against the edge of the tub, she closed her eyes.

She wasn't sure how long she'd been there, body and mind drifting in the calm, when she felt Harve slip onto the seat beside her.

"You're tense," he said. "Turn sideways just a little, and I'll give you a neck rub."

If she'd felt as if she were floating on a cloud before, the touch of his hands was heaven. She almost moaned with pleasure as he kneaded the muscles of her neck and shoulders.

His hands stilled for a moment, then began to move again, caressing now, featherlight, tempting, enticing.

"Lottie." Her name on his lips was a whisper of sound. She could no more resist the call than a creek could stop flowing. She turned in his arms.

His blue eyes seemed to glow as he said her name. Then he lowered his head, his lips seeking hers.

His kiss was slow and thoughtful. She snuggled

into his embrace and lifted her face to him in silent plea. His mouth reclaimed hers, more demanding this time, and she instinctively parted her lips under his.

With a groan that was both pleasure and frustration, he lifted his mouth from hers and gathered her closer. Her skin tingled where he touched her as she tried to force her confused emotions into order. At last, seemingly reluctantly, he loosened his hold and moved a few inches away.

"Lottie..." he said, sounding as shaken as she felt. His voice trailed into silence. Finally he spoke again, this time in a lighter tone, "If we don't get out of here, we're both going to turn into stewed prunes."

She tried to laugh, found it impossible to utter a sound, so instead, nodded in agreement. He climbed from the tub, then as if he knew the strength had seeped from her body, reached down to assist her.

Although it was a warm spring evening, the air against her damp body was cool enough to be bracing. Somehow she found the strength to stand on her own. When he wrapped a bath sheet around her shoulders, she clasped it tightly around herself and stepped back, away from his touch, afraid to discover it was his nearness and not the warm water that made her knees feel like jelly.

"Harve..." she began, searching her mind for something to say.

The look in his eyes was mesmerizing. "No. No

postmortems," he said. "Not tonight. We can discuss this later."

She nodded, as willing as he to postpone what would be an awkward conversation. "I'll get dressed so you can take me home."

They drove the short distance from Harve's farm to his grandmother's in silence. This time, when he stopped the truck, she waited until he came around to open the passenger door. He had her well trained, she realized with ironic amusement.

"I'm driving to Tulsa to look at a horse tomorrow," he said as he walked her to the door. "Would you like to come with me?"

"I can't," she said, turning to face him.

"If it's because—"

"It's because I have a lot of things to do," she told him. "I'd like to come. Really. It sounds like fun, but I simply can't."

His eyes searched her face, and then, apparently satisfied, he nodded. "Okay. Maybe another time."

"I'd like that."

"I enjoyed our day," he said.

"So did I. Thank you for all your help...and for sharing your blackberry pie."

He grinned. "You're welcome to share my pie anytime."

"Well, I...uh, I guess I'd better go in. Good night, Harve."

He bent forward, his lips brushing her cheek. "Good night, Lottie. See you next week."

REALIZING SHE WAS apprehensive about her next meeting with Harve, Lottie tried to stay busy enough Sunday not to think of him. For the most part, her plan worked—until Abby mentioned he'd called from Tulsa to say he'd be out of town for a few days.

"I'm glad to see you and Harve spending time together," Abby said. "My grandson needs someone in his life. I think you're good for him."

"We're only friends," Lottie told her, becoming a little weary of this refrain. "Besides, we disagree a lot."

"Nothing wrong with being friends. Friendship is as important as love in a good relationship, but being friends doesn't mean you always have to agree. My Harvey and I were best friends."

Lottie sighed. She really hoped this wasn't going to be a replay of her recent conversation with Myrtle. Were the two women involved in a conspiracy to match her with Harve?

"Friends or lovers, neither requires agreeing with the other all the time," Abby went on. "It's that ability to be your own person, the freedom to disagree and to allow the person you love to disagree with you that defines a lasting relationship. My Harvey and I had that, and we had a long happy marriage."

"I'm sure you're right," Lottie interrupted, "but—"

Abby continued as if Lottie hadn't spoken. "I

don't mind telling you, I worried about Rosemary and my grandson. I don't believe they had that type of bond.''

"We shouldn't be discussing this," Lottie said gently.

"I don't see why not," Abby said, refusing to be deterred. "It's all in the past now. Rosemary was sweet and gentle, but there was no challenge there. She never disagreed with Harve, never questioned his decisions, never made him stop and think. If they'd married, she would have bored him silly within six months. Now if you and Harve...well, I doubt he'd ever be bored. Neither would you."

"Harve and I don't have that kind of relationship," Lottie insisted. "We're only friends."

"Both of you are stubborn as mules," Abby said. "You think about what I said."

In spite of her efforts to dismiss the conversation, Lottie found herself replaying it in her mind. Abby was right about one thing. Harve intrigued her, beguiled her, amused her and at times infuriated her. But he never bored her.

No, it was impossible. As a couple *they* were impossible. She wouldn't allow herself to fall in love with him. It would never work. Still...

She'd be thankful when Monday morning finally arrived. The situation at work would keep her thoughts occupied with things other than Harve.

WHEN THE BANK OPENED Monday morning, Lottie could feel the enthusiasm and renewed confidence among the employees. Saturday hours could be considered a success for that reason alone.

Various chores kept her busy until young Samuel Morgan arrived for his appointment shortly after two-thirty. His father, John, had died recently, and as an only son, the young man had inherited his father's eighty-acre farm and the farm's mortgage.

"What can I do for you today, Mr. Morgan?" she asked after ushering him into her office.

She listened as he explained that last year his father's failing health had required selling off their cattle. Samuel was currently attending university, majoring in horticulture, and had a year of studies left to complete his degree. He'd started a small produce farm and greenhouse operation in specialty crops and, with his wife's assistance, currently had accounts with several area restaurants for his vegetables.

"The produce is providing living expenses," he told her, "and I'm using a combination of grants and scholarships for my college expenses. But with Dad's death, we don't have the income to make the mortgage payments."

"So what are you asking, Mr. Morgan?"

"I guess, well, we were wondering if we could refinance the farm to give us enough money to keep the mortgage payments current until I'm out of school."

"You realize the existing mortgage is an old one.

The interest rate is much lower than current rates. You'd be increasing debt, as well as costs, and your new payments would be much higher than at present."

"I know," he said, nodding, "but I don't know what else to do. I don't want to quit school, but unless I do, or until I finish, we can't increase our produce operation. My wife talked about trying to find a job, but she's doing most of the work at the farm now, so she really doesn't have the time. We thought about trying to put a few feeder beef on the pasture, but the price of beef is so low that even if we did we wouldn't see any return until we sold them in the fall."

"So essentially, you're asking the bank to lend you the money to make your mortgage payments for the next year. You'd be going further in debt every day."

"After I'm out of school and able to work at it full-time, I'm sure the greenhouse and produce operation will pay off. We could sell double our production now. I don't know what else to do, Ms. Carlyle. I don't want to quit school and I don't want to lose the farm."

Lottie could hear the despair in his voice. "Don't worry, Mr. Morgan," she said. "The current mortgage balance is much less than the value of the property. Refinancing is an option, although, under the circumstances, I'm not sure it's your best option, but we'll work something out. I promise. Let me think a moment.''

She saw some of his tension and despair fade. She leaned back in her chair, her fingers drumming idly on the desk blotter.

"You said your greenhouse and produce operation is small, is that right?''

He nodded.

"So most of your land is still in pasture—pasture that's not being used at this time?''

He nodded again.

"Have you thought about renting out the pasture to increase income flow?''

"Yes, ma'am. But with beef prices depressed, most of the ranchers have already decreased their herds to what their holdings will support. They're trying to keep their current stock, hoping prices will rise. No one's buying new stock.''

"But they're not reducing herd size, either, are they?''

"Not now. Not at the current prices. Not if they can help it.''

"I'm not a farmer or a rancher, but if I understand what you're telling me, a rancher would be better off holding on to his stock than selling. Is that correct?''

"Yes, ma'am. Right now a man will lose money on every head he sells.''

"Then I have an idea that just might solve your problem.''

She saw a ray of hope in his eyes as she explained that she happened to know a local rancher who was taking part of his pasture out of production to plant alfalfa and was planning to reduce his herd accordingly. "If it means a loss by selling now, Mr. Jamison might be interested in renting suitable pasture and keeping his stock until prices rise. He might even be interested in increasing the size of his herd, since he can now buy at low prices. Once his alfalfa field is in production, he'll be able to support the larger herd.

"I'm not going to approve your loan today, Mr. Morgan," she said. "We'll consider it again if necessary, but I think that if you can rent out the pasture, it should cover your mortgage payments. So why don't you investigate that option before we consider increasing your indebtedness?"

"I...I don't know what to say," he stammered.

She frowned. "It doesn't sound like a feasible plan to you?"

"No. That's not what I meant. It sounds good. What I don't understand is...well, I guess I thought the bank would jump at the chance to refinance the loan and raise my interest rates. Isn't that what banks do? Try to make more money?"

"Yes," she said, "within certain parameters, which frankly, Mr. Morgan, you don't meet at the present time. The worth of your property is certainly high enough to qualify for a larger mortgage, but we need to look at ability to repay, and right now you don't have sufficient cash flow to assume higher repayment costs."

Samuel Morgan shifted in his chair, the worried look back on his face. "But you said the decision not to increase the loan wasn't final."

"Yes, and I meant it," she told him. "As a small independent bank, we have the flexibility of considering other factors when we approve a loan, such as potential delayed cash flow. If necessary, that's exactly the rationale I'll use to approve your loan, but I'd rather have you try to keep things together without increasing indebtedness until you're ready to increase production."

She smiled. "Your family has been a good bank customer for several generations, Mr. Morgan. When you've finished school and are ready to expand, I hope you'll come back to us for the financing."

By the time they'd finished their conversation, the bank was closed. "I don't know how to thank you," the young farmer told her as she walked with him across the lobby.

"There's nothing to thank me for," she said, "but do let me know how things work out with Mr. Jamison. If necessary, we'll work something else out."

Lottie saw him to the door and locked it behind him. A good afternoon's work, she told herself as she headed back to her office. This was what small-town banking was all about—a partnership between bank and customer for the benefit of both.

She looked at her desk, once again heaped high with papers and files, and decided to straighten up before leaving for the day.

She worked steadily for nearly half an hour, examining the stacks of paperwork, piece by piece, filing some, discarding others, until only the overflowing in-basket remained. She briefly considered leaving it until the next day, then with a sigh, pulled it in front of her. It would be worth staying a few minutes longer to come the next morning to a clean desk.

The basket was nearly empty when she saw the envelope. Plain. White. No name.

She trembled and felt the hair on the back of her neck prickle.

Nonsense, she told herself as she reached for it. Just because it looked the same didn't mean it was. In spite of her mental protests, however, she wasn't surprised when she carefully unfolded the single sheet of paper.

Like the first note, the paper was common and again the words had been cut from magazine and newspaper headlines and carefully pasted together. The message was shorter this time, but no less unpleasant:

YOU've BEEN WaRned.

# CHAPTER ELEVEN

LOTTIE LOOKED at the note, her apprehension quickly turning to frustration.

Her questions were the same as when she'd received the first note.

Who? Why?

Unfortunately the answers were no more available now then before.

In the weeks since her return to Little Falls she'd almost forgotten the first note. She'd been welcomed by most of the community, tolerated by the rest. Even the gossip resurrected about her father's crime had all but disappeared.

And now this! Just when she'd begun to believe she could build a place here.

Obviously she had an enemy.

*Don't overreact. Don't give it more importance than it deserves.* It was, after all, a message from someone too cowardly to confront her face-to-face.

The list of possible suspects flashed through her mind, slightly revised from the first time around. Although her uncle Cyrus continued to disapprove of her actions, the two of them had achieved a sort of uneasy truce. And Jeff was being cooperative.

He even seemed to endorse the changes she was instituting.

Of course, either of them might be only pretending to accept her.

No, she told herself firmly. That kind of thinking was only paranoia. She considered herself a good judge of character. She wanted to believe that neither of them would send anonymous warnings.

Someone else in the community, then? Someone angry over a slight, imagined or real? From her? Or her mother? Her father? An old affront?

That line of inquiry seemed more reasonable, especially since she'd received the first warning only days after returning to town.

But she had no way of knowing who either of her parents might have angered all those years ago. Nor was she responsible for their actions.

Should she mention the notes to anyone?

The arguments against going public were the same now as they'd been the first time around. It was unlikely the author of the note could be identified, and the resulting publicity certainly wouldn't enhance the bank's reputation or its shaky financial circumstances.

What about Harve? Could she discuss it with him? She hadn't completely trusted him before. She did now, at least in areas concerning the bank and her personal safety. He would recognize the need for discretion.

*Forget it!* He'd also wrap her in cotton wool so

tightly she wouldn't be able to breathe. Good grief, look at how he'd reacted when she had a simple could-happen-to-anyone flat tire. If he knew someone was sending her threatening notes...well, she didn't even want to think about it.

Besides, she didn't feel threatened. Perhaps she had the first time, but not now. Today's note—it was more nuisance than anything.

She laid it aside and quickly finished dealing with the remaining items from the in-basket, then surveyed her clean desktop with satisfaction. As she gathered her belongings to leave, tucking the note into her briefcase, she realized she was still carrying around the original one. She'd get rid of both of them later, she decided. There was no reason to keep them.

As she set the security alarm and let herself out the back door of the bank, she glanced at her watch. It was too late to drop in at the Down Home. Myrtle, already busy with the supper crowd, would have no time to chat. Instead, Lottie decided, she'd make a quick stop at the house to see if her kitchen appliances had been delivered. If they had, she'd be one step closer to moving into her own house.

Although she enjoyed Abby's company and appreciated the use of the apartment, Lottie knew she'd feel more settled, more in charge of her life, once she moved into her own place.

TUESDAY PROVED to be a slow day at the bank, and with time on her hands, Lottie turned again to the investment account that had intrigued her the previous week. Now she was determined to discover what was bothering her.

She started as before, slowly scrolling through the account, paying particular attention to the interest postings. Again she observed they seemed low, consistent and carefully posted.

Consistent? Too consistent?

She flicked back a screen into an earlier month, then forward again. Dear heaven, how could she have missed it?

The interest earnings were posted twice a month, on the first and the fifteenth, and they were exactly the same each month, regardless of a varying number of days in the investment periods, regardless of the additional revenues added to the totals from the previous posting.

Feeling a surge of adrenaline, she scrolled back through the last year of investment records. The pattern was the same.

Was it sloppy account posting? Or was someone hiding something?

Like diverting funds?

Like...embezzlement?

Oh, no. Her father had apparently done this. Was what she was seeing now a copycat crime?

*Don't jump to conclusions,* she cautioned herself. She'd been seventeen when her father, accused of embezzling bank funds, drove his car off a bluff and into the lake at the edge of town. She'd never seen the records that detailed her father's manipulations. She only knew they'd been considered a classic case of embezzlement: bank funds invested in short-term high-yield ventures carried in the bank portfolio as long-term low-yield investments. Funds matching the lower interest-rate earnings had been credited to the bank's accounts, and the difference between what was paid and what was posted had disappeared into an anonymous account.

If something similar was going on now, they'd have one thing in common—an account where the excess funds were being hidden. A secret account.

Lottie knew she was no computer expert, but she'd be able to spot an unauthorized account, at least she would if it was listed as a separate account.

An hour later she gave up. If there was an account, it was hidden and she didn't have the expertise to find it.

*Slow down, Lottie. Maybe there is no secret account. Maybe there's a simple explanation for the uniform postings.*

Like what?

How could she find out? Who should she ask? If she was right, in her ignorance she might ask exactly the wrong person.

Maybe she was letting her imagination run away with her.

Maybe.

But the more she thought about it, the more convinced she was that her first impression was correct.

*Someone's embezzling bank funds.*

She took a deep breath. *Okay. Don't panic. Exactly what do I have?*

Not much, she admitted. Only a gut feeling and a suspicious-looking investment posting that dated back at least a year. Certainly not enough to justify calling in the authorities. Besides, the last thing the bank needed was another scandal.

Not that she'd have much choice if she was right, but first she had to be sure.

Exactly how far back did the pattern go? That should be her first order of business. To examine the records, she needed to dig into the archives in the basement vault.

She'd have to be careful. She certainly didn't want the wrong person curious as to why she was poking around in old files. She also needed to find the documentation on the investments. The computer postings were only an extract of account activity. There should be documents somewhere, paper files identifying the investment funds and the interest percentage due.

Maybe when she found them, they'd prove she had an overactive imagination. She wished she could believe it.

If only she could discuss it with someone.

If Cyrus or Jeff weren't her prime suspects, they'd be the most logical choices. It was Cyrus who'd given her the information on early-with-drawal penalties for this account. Didn't that indicate he probably knew what was going on? *If* anything was going on?

And Jeff, well, he was Cyrus's son. Even if he wasn't involved, she doubted he'd be able to conceal his suspicions from his father. He wasn't good at hiding his feelings.

*Hold it! Slow down,* she ordered herself. Theoretically Cyrus and Jeff might be prime suspects, but everyone who worked in the bank had access to the computer.

She certainly couldn't discuss her suspicions with anyone outside the board. She didn't know Andrew Pettigrew well enough to predict how he would react, and she didn't want to upset Abby. That left only Harve.

No, she couldn't go to Harve. He'd either think she was imagining things or, more likely, come charging in like a bull in a china shop, determined to put everything to rights.

So she was on her own. At least for now. The one thing she could do was document what she'd found and what she was doing.

She slipped a disk into the computer and copied the investment file, then wrote a brief explanation of the day's discoveries and what she planned to do. If she kept a daily journal and created a separate file for each entry, the disk would show the date and time the file was saved. She knew it wasn't much in the way of documentation, but under the circumstances, it seemed the best she could do.

Her next step would be to examine the old account records and she'd need to do that after-hours.

Lottie sighed. Everything would be so much simpler if she was living in her own home.

Why not? she thought with sudden inspiration. Although the renovation work wasn't finished, it was close enough to completion that, by restricting herself to only two or three rooms, she'd be comfortable enough. Then she could come and go at the bank without attracting attention—especially if she limited her search time to daylight hours. Lights shining from the basement after dark would tend to cause comment.

Saturday afternoon! After the bank closed. It was perfect. No one would comment if she was the last one to leave. She often was. And if her few extra minutes turned into a few extra hours, no one would know.

She'd spend after-hours the rest of the week getting settled in at her house. That would give Abby several days to get used to her moving out. The old woman might privately object, but she wouldn't protest. Living at Abby's house had always been considered a temporary measure.

It would work, Lottie thought and, for the first time since her earlier discovery, began to feel better.

HARVE RETURNED from his trip to Tulsa feeling good. He wanted to see Lottie, to resume their courtship dance. It had begun the day she'd returned to town, although it had taken him a while to admit it.

He was facing reality now.

He was falling in love.

And if he'd correctly interpreted her response to him, the feeling was mutual.

He waltzed into the Down Home feeling as cheerful as a crow in a corncrib. Even Myrtle commented on his good mood.

Then he heard that Lottie had turned down Samuel Morgan's request for a loan.

Why?

Harve thought he knew Lottie, thought he understood her, had convinced himself that her return to Little Falls was an unexpected boon for the bank and the community. He'd thought they shared similar interests, similar goals, a basic philosophy.

He'd even lost his earlier concerns that she wouldn't fit into the community, that in her years away from Little Falls she'd adopted the philosophy of her big-city banking cohorts—ignoring the needs of the customer in pursuit of profit.

Now he was afraid he'd made a mistake. Had he been too quick to dismiss these concerns?

Samuel Morgan was an honest, intelligent and enterprising young man. His family had successfully worked the same farm for generations. He would have been good for the loan on only a signature, but with the family farm as security, there was no reason for her to turn down his application.

So why had she said no?

Maybe he was wrong. Maybe she did have a reason for denying the loan, although he couldn't imagine what it was. One thing was certain: he needed to find out.

Half an hour later he was sitting in his truck outside her house wondering about the best way to approach her.

There wasn't a best way, he decided. Whatever he asked, however he asked it, she was going to accuse him of interfering.

And she'd be right.

But he wasn't going to stand by and watch the young man lose the family farm because the bank was too shortsighted to advance him the funds needed to get through a bad spell. If necessary, he'd make Samuel a personal loan.

Harve climbed out of the truck and headed for Lottie's back door. Maybe she did have a rational explanation. He owed her the chance to express it. He was determined to be calm, reasonable, sensible.

His resolution lasted until he saw the collection of boxes stacked haphazardly on the back porch. One large box propped open the screen door, allowing unrestricted entry into the kitchen. Like the porch, the room resembled a war zone. Stacks of boxes and crates covered every inch of counter space. Packing supplies spilled onto the floor like toys from a child's play box. What in hell was she doing?

"Lottie?" he yelled, stepping into the kitchen.

There was a rustling sound from the far side of the room before her head popped into view from behind a stack of boxes.

"Harve? What are you doing here? I thought you were in Tulsa."

Her flushed cheeks and her tousled hair made him think of soft pillows and satin sheets, but it was the warmth and welcome in her voice and the smile on her lips that had him scrambling to control his accelerating heartbeat.

He cleared his throat and swallowed. "What's going on here?"

Her smile faltered. "I'm unpacking."

"Unpacking? Surely you're not thinking of moving in. The house isn't finished."

"Near enough for my purposes," she told him, her gaze searching his face. "What's wrong?"

"I don't think you should move in yet."

"And I disagree." She sighed. "Why are you here, Harve? What's bothering you? You haven't come looking for me to tell me I shouldn't move—it's obvious you didn't know."

So much for hiding his feelings, he thought. "I did have a question to ask you," he said finally. "Why did you turn down Samuel Morgan's request for a loan?"

She went still, shoulders stiffening, all animation fleeing from her face. "Have you talked to him? Did he tell you that?"

"No."

"Then I guess the grapevine's working overtime again." He could hear the resignation in her voice.

"Lottie, I only want to know—"

"I do not discuss the private business of bank customers with *anyone*," she said coolly. "If Mr. Morgan wishes to do so, that's his business. Now if that's all…"

"I'm only trying to understand why—"

"I'm sure if you go back to your source, he or she will have an explanation. Or you might try talking to Mr. Morgan, assuming he's willing to discuss his private business with you. As far as I'm concerned, the subject is closed. You'll have to excuse me now, Harve. As you can see I'm busy. You know the way out."

Before he could protest she'd turned her back on him, picked up a box and disappeared into another part of the house.

Dammit! He'd certainly handled that with finesse—landed himself neck deep in a pit of manure. Even with luck and divine intervention he wondered how long it would take to dig himself out.

FIGHTING TEARS, Lottie left the kitchen. She'd been so happy to see him. And then, even if he hadn't exactly criticized her, the accusation had been in his voice if not in his words.

How could he? Although she'd known from the beginning he was reserving judgment on her competence, she'd thought that in the time they'd spent together he had developed a respect for her.

She could understand his being upset if she had, in fact, denied young Morgan's request for a loan. But to turn on her simply because of idle gossip...

Darn him, anyway. She wasn't going to let him upset her. She *wasn't*.

She leaned against the wall, holding the box on one hip and swiping at her eyes with the back of her free hand, as she heard the sound of his truck driving away.

## CHAPTER TWELVE

LOTTIE SHUFFLED file folders on her desk and tried to appear busy as she listened impatiently to the sounds of Jeff and Josephine closing up. The bank's second Saturday morning of operation had, if anything, been as busy as their first. Heavy foot traffic was no proof of success, but it was a good indicator. If participation meant anything, the residents of Little Falls were endorsing the bank's expanded hours with enthusiasm.

She'd spent last night in her own bed, in her own house. Although the move from Abby's to town had kept her distracted enough and physically tired enough to prevent her from brooding about her last meeting with Harve when he'd stormed into her kitchen three nights ago, it wasn't enough to completely banish him from her thoughts.

*You overreacted. He caught you by surprise and you attacked.*

Not that Harve was completely blameless. He'd made no attempt to approach her with either tact or diplomacy.

Enough. She didn't have time to examine her reaction to him. Or his to her. Not now.

She listened as Jeff told Josephine goodbye, then heard the sound of the front door being locked. She lifted a document from one of the files on her desk and pretended to be reading it.

"Are you about ready to call it a day?" Jeff asked from her office's open doorway.

"I'm going to be a little while," she told him. "I want to finish proofreading this agreement. I'll need it first thing Monday. You go on."

"Are you sure? I'll stay if I can be of help."

"Thanks, but there's nothing I need you to do," she assured him. "Go home. I won't be long. You can set the master alarm and I'll let myself out the back way."

She listened to Jeff moving around in the office next to hers, then heard him walk across the lobby. The muted chimes of the Seth Thomas wall clock in the boardroom rang out the half hour.

"Door alarms are set," Jeff called. "Have a good weekend, Lottie."

"You, too. Tell Jeannie I said hello."

She waited another few minutes, in case Jeff had forgotten something and decided to come back, but when she heard the boardroom clock chime the quarter hour, decided she'd delayed long enough.

She wished she'd been able to discuss her plans for this afternoon with Harve. Then she told herself she wouldn't have discussed it with him, anyway. She didn't know enough. Not yet.

Picking up the tote bag she'd packed this morning, she went into the rest room, removed her heels, skirt and half-slip. She pulled a pair of jeans on over her hose, then added cotton socks, a pair of canvas sneakers and a sweatshirt over her blouse. It might be spring, but the basement would be cool.

She hung her suit jacket and skirt in the closet in her office, stuffed her purse and the tote bag into a bottom drawer of her desk, then grabbed her brief-case, flipped off the light and closed the door to her office.

She almost tiptoed across the lobby toward the back of the bank, then laughed at her foolishness. There was no reason to be so quiet. She was alone. Besides, she had every right to be here, every right to go into the basement.

She turned on the light switch, the bulb only dimly illuminating the basement, then closed the door behind her and descended the wooden stairs. The bank had stood in the same location since the days of its original construction. The basement, a ten-foot-deep hole in the ground, with walls of lo-cally quarried granite block covered by locally milled wide-plank boarding, was part of the original building. Tucked into one corner was a small room with double walls and what had once been a clev-erly concealed door.

When the bank first opened in June 1854, a new steel safe, complete with turn-wheel locking mech-anism, had stood in the office of the bank president, safely removed from the public, but nonetheless visible to bank customers from the lobby. It had been an excellent showpiece, a visual promise that the Little Falls bank safeguarded its customers' money with only the best, most advanced modern equipment.

Lottie always laughed when she thought of that sleight of hand by her ancestor. The modern steel safe upstairs had indeed safely protected a small amount of currency and gold, usually the day's projected needs. It was that safe, in fact, that had thwarted a robbery by the James gang in the 1870s. When the gang tried to shoot off the lock, the bullets had ricocheted harmlessly, one on them splintering a panel of the office's dark mahogany wainscoting. Even if the robbers had been successful in opening the safe, their take would have been small. It was the basement vault that securely and secretly housed the bank's valuables from fire, theft and man-made or natural disaster.

In a later building renovation, the damaged panel was removed from the president's office and reinstalled in the lobby—a reminder to its customers that the bank had successfully thwarted the notorious Jesse James.

Over the years the concealed basement vault had received a number of security improvements. First, a large hand-hammered iron hasp and padlock had been added to the door; later, a collapsible steel grille, similar to those used on open elevators in the early part of the century. The most recent addition was a complicated combination lock.

But then, during the bank's last remodeling, a modern electronically protected walk-in vault was built on the street floor, and the old basement vault was reborn as the bank's archives.

Lottie noted that the padlock and the combination lock had been removed from the vault door, although both the hasp and grille remained. The steel grille was pushed to one side, but because of the necessary climate control, the heavy door was shut.

She pulled the door open, reached inside to activate the switch for the bare lightbulb hanging from the ceiling, then entered the vault and pulled the door closed behind her.

Ledgers and papers, dating from the bank's inception, were stored in file cabinets and on shelves. The room also contained a microfiche-storage cabinet, which Lottie suspected contained copies of the original records stored on the shelves, and a newer-looking computer-disk-storage file. A table in the center of the room held both a computer terminal and a microfiche reader.

She glanced at the old ledgers on the shelves and made a mental note to spend some time examining them. But not today. Today she was interested in more recent history.

She started with the most recent computer records and worked backward. After a while, she moved from computer to microfiche, carefully examining the bank's investment accounts, forcing herself to stay calm and focused, trying to absorb what she was seeing without responding emotionally.

Finally she stood up and stretched, then walked over to the shelves and selected several volumes from the collection of ledgers. She'd already examined the microfiche from the same period, but she wanted to be sure the microfiche were true and correct copies of the original records.

A few minutes later, after replacing the ledgers on the shelf, she slumped in the chair and closed her eyes. She'd traced the investment pattern back over five years, then examined the records involved in her father's embezzlement.

She'd been right to worry. The patterns were all but identical. No wonder the bank was in trouble. Someone was copying her father's crime.

Or was "copying" the right word?

Her mind buzzed. William Carlyle had been accused of embezzlement, but not convicted. His guilt had gone unproved, but the method of his death was considered a confession of guilt.

Her mother always insisted her father was innocent. Lottie had questioned that reasoning. If he'd been innocent, why had he committed suicide?

Now she was having second thoughts.

What if her mother had been right all along? What if the current thief wasn't copying her father?

What if it was merely the original embezzler operating again?

But if that was true, why had her father committed suicide?

Or had he?

Dear heaven. Maybe she'd been blaming her father all these years for something he didn't do. Maybe his death had been a tragic accident.

Or a deliberate murder.

No. She couldn't afford to start thinking along those lines. Not now. She had to concentrate on the current crime. There was no longer any doubt. Someone was stealing from the bank.

Maybe once the thief was identified, her other questions would be answered. If not, well, she'd think about them then. First she had to tell authorities of her suspicions.

Who should she call? Little Falls police chief Billy Bob Simpson? Or Eldon Wiley, the county sheriff? Either or both? Oh, Lord, she could imagine the turf war that would cause. Besides, she wondered if either had the necessary expertise. A banking auditor, then? Or federal authorities? The FBI?

*Harve would know.*

Lottie sighed. She really had no choice. A thief, either old or new, was stealing from the bank. As a board member not directly working in the bank, Harve was the logical person to trust with the information.

Should she tell him the embezzlement pattern

she'd uncovered was almost identical to her father's? If Harve started thinking along those lines, he was too intelligent not to question the manner of her father's death.

Just as she was questioning it.

An official investigation would identify the similarities; professional investigators always looked for a pattern. They would certainly look at another embezzlement less than fifteen years old in the same bank. They would see the parallel even more quickly than she had. After all, they were experts. And they would draw the same conclusions she had: that the embezzler was either a copycat or a repeat offender.

So, she'd keep her suspicions to herself, at least for the present, and let the experts work.

Before leaving, she checked to make sure she'd refiled the records correctly, then picked up her briefcase and pushed the vault door, expecting it to swing open as easily as it had when she'd let herself in.

It didn't budge.

She tried again, harder this time. It still refused to move.

She set down her briefcase and, using both hands, shoved with all her might. The result was the same. Nothing.

Fighting a growing anxiety, telling herself that the door was heavy, that she only needed to push harder, she tried again and again, growing more frantic with each attempt.

Finally she slumped against the door and accepted the situation. She was trapped inside the vault.

HARVE WAS LOOKING for Lottie. He owed her an apology. A big apology.

He'd jumped to conclusions over the Morgan loan. He should have known better. He couldn't remember another time he'd reacted to town gossip so quickly and so blindly.

*Just goes to show how deep she is under my skin,* he thought. *Like an itch I can't reach.*

It had taken him until this morning to track down Samuel Morgan. When he'd finally located the young farmer hard at work in his greenhouse, Samuel was more than willing to discuss his dealings with the Little Falls bank and with the bank's new vice president.

"She was great, Mr. Tremayne," Samuel told him. "Said she didn't want me to go more in debt if I didn't have to, but if there was no other way, she'd approve a loan based on 'delayed anticipated revenues,' or something like that. I didn't exactly understand the jargon, but the bottom line was I'd be better off if I could hang on for the year with the old loan."

He moved a flat of bedding plants to the shady side of the greenhouse. "I already knew that, of

course, but I didn't see any other way. Then she
gave me a couple of suggestions and told me to
come back if they didn't work out. Maybe I
shouldn't tell you, Mr. Tremayne, you being a
stockholder and all, but the bank lost money not
making that loan. I'd have made good on it all right,
but the interest rate now is higher than when Dad
borrowed.''

"So the alternative suggestions she made, they
worked out all right?" Harve asked.

"Sure did. I didn't think anyone would be interested in renting pasture, not the way the beef market
is now, but I didn't know Tom Jamison was going
to have to reduce his herd size because he was reducing pasture. She told me to check with him and
see if he was interested. He jumped at the chance.
The rent revenues will let me keep up with the
mortgage payments until I'm out of school and
ready to expand. You know, I didn't expect her to
be so savvy about farming and ranching and things
like that, being from Saint Louis and all. But she
knew what she was talking about. She's a real smart
lady.''

"Yes, she is," Harve agreed.

Samuel studied his feet for a moment. Harve
could almost see him gathering his courage before
speaking again. Young Morgan might not be sea-
soned, but there was nothing wrong with his courage.

"Mind if I ask you a question, Mr. Tremayne?"

"Of course not. If I don't want to answer, I won't." Harve smiled to soften the effect of his words.

"Well, I kind of wonder what you're doing out here. Asking about the loan, I mean."

"Quite honestly, Samuel, I got hold of the wrong end of the stick. I was going to offer to finance you personally if you hadn't been able to make arrangements with the bank. Obviously you've got everything under control, although the offer stands if you ever need it. Your father wanted you to finish school. And I think you've got the beginnings of a good operation here."

"You thought the bank wouldn't help?"

"I *heard* the bank wouldn't help," he corrected.

"You heard? You mean people are saying the bank turned me down?"

"That's what I heard," Harve repeated.

"Oh, damn. That's my fault. When I came out of the bank, someone—I don't even remember who—asked me if I'd gotten the new loan. All I said was no. I was thinking about other things. I bet they're bad-mouthing Ms. Carlyle, too, aren't they?"

"There's some talk," Harve admitted.

"Well, I'll take care of that," Samuel said. "Got to go into town, anyway. While I'm there, I'll mention what a good job Ms. Carlyle did in helping me *not* need a new loan. Reckon that'll do it? Or should I maybe go into detail?"

"I think your general satisfaction with Ms. Carlyle and the bank will be enough," Harve said. "Your private business is your private business. The Little Falls grapevine is a hardy variety. It survives, in fact it thrives, on very little substance."

Samuel laughed. "Ain't it the truth. Thanks for dropping by, Mr. Tremayne," he said, offering his hand.

"You're welcome," Harve told him, shaking it. "Thank you for confiding in me. You could have told me it was none of my business."

"Yeah, well, my dad always said you were a smart honest man and a good friend. I figured if you were asking, you had a reason."

Harve had driven away from the Morgan ranch, impressed by the young man and feeling good about what he'd learned.

It was a unique feeling, he realized. He would admit to being wrong on occasion, but for the life of him, he couldn't remember a previous incident when he'd actually felt good about it. Just showed how proficient Lottie Carlyle was in turning his life upside down.

He glanced at his watch, realized that it was already past noon and that he'd missed her at the bank. So where was she likely to be?

When he'd stopped by his grandmother's earlier that morning, she'd told him Lottie had moved into her house in town. The house was probably his best bet. Ironic, wasn't it, he thought, how anxious he was to eat crow.

He wasn't concerned when he found no sign of her car and the house locked up tight. Okay, she'd probably stayed in town to run a few errands. He could wait until she showed up or go on into town to look for her.

The idea of confronting her with other people around had appeal. He knew she was furious with him. An audience just might temper her anger when he found her.

The first thing he noticed when he drove down Main Street was her car still parked in front of the bank. He pulled the truck into an adjacent parking space and got out. The bank was dark, as he'd known it would be, but she was obviously nearby. Maybe she was visiting Myrtle at the Down Home.

When he walked into the café, a quick glance around told him she wasn't here, either. He dropped onto a stool at the end of the counter and waited for Myrtle to notice him. It didn't take long.

"Hey, Harve. Haven't seen you in a few days. What'll you have?"

"A cup of coffee and a slice of that cherry pie," he said. "How's it going?"

"Can't complain," she told him, putting a mug of coffee on the counter in front of him. "Let me get this luncheon order up, then I'll get your pie."

He sipped his coffee, watching as Myrtle carried a tray of sandwiches to a table of strangers sitting in the corner. Back behind the counter, she lifted a piece of pie onto a plate.

"Want it à la mode?"

When he nodded, she added a scoop of vanilla ice cream. "Here you are. You in town for any special reason?"

"A piece of your pie is a good enough reason," he said with a grin, "but as a matter of fact, I'm looking for Lottie. Has she been in?"

Myrtle frowned. "Haven't seen hide nor hair of her since Monday. Been kinda looking for her, too. Had something I wanted to ask her."

He looked around to see if anyone was in easy listening distance. Satisfied he could speak without fear of being overheard, he leaned across the counter. "About the Morgan loan, I'll bet."

"Well, I wouldn't have asked outright, if you know what I mean. That's personal business between young Morgan and the bank. But I'll admit I was hoping she'd say something. The talk's getting nasty, Harve."

Harve winced at the reminder, probably unintentional, of how he'd blotted his copybook with Lottie. Even Myrtle, who wasn't afraid to talk to anyone about anything, had enough sense not to tackle a subject that was, strictly speaking, private business.

"It's a tempest in a teapot, Myrtle. I talked with Samuel this morning. He's singing Lottie's praises.

Says her advice helped him avoid taking on a bigger loan.''

Myrtle sighed in relief. ''I didn't want to believe the talk, you know, but I've kept my mouth shut 'cause I haven't heard any different. But if that's what he's saying, I just might happen to mention I heard it.''

''Great,'' he said. ''In fact, when Samuel heard about the story going around, he said he'd be in town later today and straighten it out.''

She nodded, then glanced at his empty pie plate. ''You want another piece? Or something else? It won't be the first time I've fed you dinner after dessert.''

''Thanks, but not today. I still need to find Lottie. She's not out at her house. The bank's closed, but her car's still parked there. Got any ideas where she might be?''

''None that I can think of,'' Myrtle said, then frowned. ''Unless she went home with Jeff for lunch. She and Jeannie have become pretty good friends. Maybe Jeff said he'd be coming back to town, so there was no reason to take both cars.''

''Well, it's an idea, anyway. Thanks, Myrtle. You take care.''

He debated for a moment whether to call or drive out to Jeff and Jeannie's place, then decided to go in person.

The trip proved as futile as his other stops.

''When I left, she was still working in her office," Jeff told him. "She said she'd only be a few more minutes." He glanced at his watch. "It's been a couple of hours. I doubt she's still there, but she might be. If you knock on the front door, she might not hear you if she's in her office, but you could go down the alley and knock on her office window."

"The silent alarm won't go off?" Harve asked.

"Not if you only knock. Don't try opening it, though."

Harve thanked him and drove back downtown. He knocked on Lottie's office window, but knew, even as he did, she wasn't there. He could see through the window that the office was empty, the lights were off and the door closed.

He walked around the bank again, checking to see if her car was still there. Then he dropped into every business office along the two-block downtown business strip. No one had seen her all day, unless they'd been in the bank during morning banking hours.

Now he was beginning to worry. It was nearly four in the afternoon, and apparently no one had seen her since shortly after noon when Jeff left the bank.

He stopped by Clyde's to see if she'd reported a problem with the car.

"Of course not, Mr. Tremayne. If she had, I wouldn't have left it just sitting there on the street. I'd have towed it in to see what was wrong."

"That's what I thought," Harve said, "but her car's just sitting there and no one seems to have seen her, so I thought I'd double-check."

"Well, if I see her or hear from her, I'll sure let you know. Tell her you're looking for her, too."

"Thanks, Clyde. I'd appreciate it."

He drove back to her house and found it locked up as tightly as it had been when he'd stopped by earlier. Then he got in the truck and went back to Jeff's.

"Something's wrong," he said. "No one has seen her all afternoon. Her car's still parked at the bank, but her office is dark. I've checked all over town and out at her house. You were the last person to see her."

"You're really worried, aren't you?"

"I passed worried about an hour ago."

"I can't imagine what she'd still be doing at the bank, but let's go see. If you're worried, I've got an idea I should be, too."

Jeff drove his own car downtown, parking beside Harve's truck. "The front-door alarm's set for the weekend," he said. "We need to go in the back."

Harve stood to one side as Jeff tested the back-door alarm. "I locked it when I left," he said. "When she left, she reset it—if she left. There's no way to tell."

He turned off the alarm and gestured for Harve to go in, then followed, resetting the lock as soon as he was inside. "Lottie! Hey, Lottie, you still in here?" he called.

The only answer was silence.

"Okay," Jeff said, "let's look around."

"What about the alarms?"

"We don't have motion detectors," Jeff told him. "As long as you don't touch the front or back doors, you'll be fine."

They walked across the lobby together. "I'll take the rest rooms," Jeff said. "You check her office. No, wait a minute. I'll have to get the master key. Lottie always locks her office before she leaves."

Impatient, Harve reached for the office door. The knob turned easily in his hand.

"That's funny," Jeff said. "As I said, she always locks her office."

Harve was growing more uneasy with every passing second. He stepped into the room. Jeff pushed past him and hit the enter button on her computer. A screen proclaiming MAIN MENU flashed into view. "She logged off her computer," he said.

"I don't know what I'm looking for," Harve said as he started pulling open desk drawers. A center keyhole drawer contained the usual assortment of pencils, pens and paper clips; the top drawer on the left, various stationery supplies. The right-hand drawer seemed to be devoted to typewriter and computer manuals. He pulled open the bottom drawer and froze.

"Jeff, is this Lottie's purse?" he asked, his voice shaky as he lifted it from the drawer.

"It sure looks like it," Jeff said softly, his face turning pale.

Harve unfastened the catch and pulled out Lottie's wallet. "She might go off without her car, but she wouldn't leave her purse. Dammit, where is she?"

"She has to be here somewhere. We'll find her. I'll check the rest rooms."

"What about the basement?"

"That's an idea," Jeff said, his voice suddenly lighter. "The bank's archives are in the old vault. If she was examining old records down there, she wouldn't hear us call. The walls are thick, and she'd have the door closed. It's climate-controlled."

"You get the rest rooms. I'll check downstairs," Harve said, already on his way out of the office.

"The light switch is on the left at the top of the stairs," Jeff called after him.

Harve opened the door to the basement and felt his heart rate begin to slow. The light was already on. "Lottie," he called out as he started down the stairs. "Are you down here?"

He thought he heard a thump but couldn't be sure. He walked to the old vault, saw the door was closed, the iron hasp secured by a bolt. She couldn't be in there, not with the door fastened from the outside.

"Lottie," he called again, turning away from the vault door.

The thumping sound came again.

Spinning around, he grabbed the bolt from the lock hasp, dropping it in his haste as he pulled at the vault door. It swung open easily.

"Harve." Lottie threw herself at him so forcefully he staggered back a step. "Thank God," she said, throwing her arms around his neck. "I've never been so happy to see anyone in my life."

He wrapped his arms around her protectively. "Are you all right?" he asked, his voice husky.

"I am now. When the door stuck, I thought I'd be in there all weekend."

"Stuck? Lottie, that door wasn't stuck. It was locked."

She loosened her hold on him and stepped back, her eyes wide. "Locked! But how? Who?"

"That's what I'd like to know," he said grimly, and stooped down to pick up the bolt.

"Hey, Harve," Jeff called from the top of the stairs, "did you find her? Is she all right?"

"Jeff's here, too?" Lottie asked.

"How do you think I got in?" He turned toward the stairs. "I found her, Jeff. She—"

"The door to the vault was stuck," Lottie called out, and threw Harve a pleading look not to contradict her. "I'm fine, Jeff, but I sure am glad to see you two."

"The door stuck?" Jeff hurried down the basement stairs. "You could have been in there until Monday."

"Believe me, I know."

When Harve dropped the bolt into his jacket pocket, he heard her breathe a soft sigh.

Jeff looked at her jeans and sweatshirt suspiciously. "What's going on, Lottie? I thought you were only going to finish proofreading a document."

"That's all I planned to do," she told him. "Then I discovered I needed to check the old agreement. It wasn't in my files. I knew I could find a copy down here."

"And just happened to have a change of clothes with you?" Jeff didn't bother to disguise his disbelief.

"As a matter of fact, I did. I brought them to work with me last week, planning to do some research down here. I just hadn't got around to it. Thank goodness I had them. It's cool in there. If I hadn't changed, I would have been frozen."

Jeff's look of disbelief changed to one of concern. "Are you sure you're all right?"

"I'm fine. Really. Just a little chilly and tired."

"Ready to go home?" Harve asked her quietly.

She ducked into the vault and picked up her briefcase. "Yes, I am definitely ready to go home," she told him.

Jeff switched off the light in the vault, then swung the door open and shut a couple of times. "The door seems to be working all right now. I don't understand it. There's no latch and it's never stuck before."

"Maybe it's harder to open from the inside."

"If it stuck once, it could stick again," Jeff said to no one in particular. "Monday morning I'll call and get an emergency phone installed in there. Just in case."

Loath to leave Lottie alone, Harve walked her back to her office. He waited as she retrieved her suit from the closet and her purse and tote bag from her desk, then they rejoined Jeff at the rear door.

"Thank you for coming," she told Jeff.

"I'm glad Harve insisted on checking in the bank," he said. "When I think of your being stuck in there…"

"Don't think about it," she said with a shiver. "I'm trying not to."

"Do you feel up to driving to your place?" Harve asked after Jeff drove away. "You can leave your car there, shower, grab a change of clothes, and then we'll go out to the farm."

"I don't think—"

"We need to talk, Lottie, but coming with me is not a matter for discussion. Someone deliberately locked you in that vault. If I hadn't been looking for you… Well, I'm not going to leave you alone.

We can stay at your place or mine. Your choice, but your presence at my farm will create less talk than if I'm at your house." He held her car door open for her. "Now get in. I'll follow you."

This time she didn't argue.

## CHAPTER THIRTEEN

HARVE WAS RIGHT, Lottie knew. They did need to talk. Checking her rearview mirror, she felt a rush of relief when she identified his truck behind her.

What if he hadn't come looking for her? She gripped the steering wheel tightly, trying to control her trembling hands.

Someone had locked her in the vault!

*Don't think about it. Not now,* she ordered herself. *Just drive.*

Funny how the town looked so normal—like any other late Saturday afternoon. She'd seen it all before, a hundred, a thousand times. There was Clyde's garage on the left, both pump islands occupied. Charlie Zimmermann's barbershop seemed to be doing a booming business. Isaac Easton's general store had its share of weekend shoppers, too.

She wondered if she'd ever be able to view the small town the same way again.

But Little Falls wasn't to blame, she realized. No anonymous town resident could have locked her in the vault. Only someone with access to the bank could have trapped her that way.

That certainly narrowed the list of suspects.

The one thing she didn't have to wonder about was why. Her discovery today answered that question. Whoever it was was trying to scare her. It was a warning.

She wouldn't have died in there, not between now and Monday. The vault wasn't airtight. There was plenty of oxygen. She would have been cold, but not cold enough to have developed hypothermia.

She would have been extremely hungry and thirsty, too, but no one starved to death or died of thirst in less than two days, did they?

Would her jailer have snuck in early Monday morning and removed the lock? Maybe. It would certainly have made her look like a hysterical fool.

*Stop thinking about it,* she ordered herself again. *Think about getting home and taking a nice hot shower.*

Then she'd talk to Harve.

She let out a sigh of relief when she turned into the long winding driveway leading to the back of her house. Then she leaned her head against the seat and closed her eyes. When Harve's truck pulled up beside her, she gathered her belongings and climbed out.

Harve was silent as he followed her onto the porch. He waited while she dug in her purse for the back-door key.

The kitchen looked exactly as she'd left it this morning—a lifetime ago. Strange. For some reason she expected it to seem different. She gave herself a mental shake and turned to face Harve, plastering a smile on her face she knew must look forced.

"The living room isn't finished yet," she said. "Can you wait in here?"

She took his grunt for agreement and continued through the kitchen toward the staircase. She felt his presence one step behind her and turned to face him.

"What are you doing?"

"Going upstairs with you."

"I know we have to talk, Harve. I agreed to go out to the farm with you. I'm not trying to escape," she said, her exasperation overcoming fatigue.

"Dammit, Lottie, I'm trying to protect you. Someone deliberately locked you in the bank vault."

"You think whoever did it is upstairs waiting for me?" she asked incredulously. "For heaven's sake, there's no one here. The door was locked."

"So was the bank," he said softly.

She grabbed the banister, the truth of his words and the realization of her vulnerability making her knees like spaghetti.

He caught her under the elbow, his touch firm and warm and reassuring. "I'm sorry, Lottie. I didn't mean to frighten you, but you need to be cautious. I agree it's unlikely anyone's in the house, but I'll feel better knowing for sure. Let me check it out."

When she managed to nod weakly, he brushed past her. She heard him enter her bedroom, open and shut the closet door, then the adjoining bathroom. Finally he went along the upstairs hall, opening and closing the doors to each of the remaining rooms.

"Okay, all clear," he said, appearing at the top of the stair landing. "Enjoy your shower. I'll wait in the kitchen. Is it all right if I make a pot of coffee?"

"Of course. I'll try to hurry," she said, surprised her vocal cords seemed to be working normally.

"Take your time and try to relax." He paused on the step above her, reaching out to brush a strand of hair from her forehead. "It's over. You're safe now and I'm going to see you stay that way."

By the time she was ready to join Harve downstairs, Lottie was feeling much better. She'd admit to being scared when Harve rescued her this afternoon. Discovering evidence of an embezzlement, getting stuck in the vault and then finding that someone had deliberately locked you in was enough to scare anyone. But the shower had done its job. She felt ready to face the world—and Harve.

She paused at the kitchen door, studying him. He was sitting at the kitchen table, his back to her, apparently deep in thought. Dressed in his usual jeans and yoked cowboy shirt, he looked solid and dependable—like a lifeline in turbulent waters.

Somehow she knew he would help get her through this.

She must have made a sound because he turned suddenly, then smiled.

"I didn't hear you come down," he said. "Do you want a cup of coffee or are you ready to go?"

"Are you sure…" She hesitated.

"That you're going home with me? Absolutely. We're going out to the farm and we'll raid the fridge for whatever goodies Annie left. Then we're going to talk."

She nodded.

"Before we leave," he went on, "there's one thing I'd like to say."

She looked at him, puzzled.

"I want to apologize for our last meeting. I should've had my facts straight."

It took her a moment to figure out what he was talking about. "Oh, you mean the Morgan loan."

"Right. I'm sorry, Lottie. I had no business asking you about it. You were right—it was Morgan's private business. Lord knows, I should never have listened to the grapevine."

"It's all right, Harve. I overreacted, too."

He shook his head. "The only thing I'm glad about is that I needed to apologize. If I hadn't been looking for you·this afternoon, I wouldn't have realized you were missing. Incidentally young Morgan is singing your praises. I suspect there'll be an entirely new story circulating on the grapevine by tomorrow.''

"You wanted to apologize? That's why you were looking for me?''

"Uh-huh.''

"Then I'll be eternally grateful for our misunderstanding,'' she told him, determined to keep the tone light. "Have I said thank-you for the rescue?''

"That's not necessary.'' He smiled. "Now let's go see what kind of culinary delights Annie left for us. I told her you were mad at me and I doubted you'd be out this weekend, but she, at least, has faith in my ability to calm troubled waters. 'Miss Lottie's not one to hold a grudge,' she told me. 'And if she does, try bribery. You tell her I fixed one of her favorites.'''

"That sounds like Annie,'' Lottie said, laughing.

"I like to hear you laugh,'' he told her.

"Amazing I can, considering the sort of day I've had.''

At the farm they followed Harve's previously planned itinerary, a quiet dinner consisting of garden-fresh peas, sliced country ham, a macaroni-and-cheese casserole and a tossed salad of garden greens.

"I don't believe it,'' Harve teased. "I actually bribed you with a macaroni-and-cheese casserole. You're a cheap date, Ms. Carlyle.''

"One of *Annie's* macaroni-and-cheese casseroles," she corrected. "It was one of my favorite meals as a child."

"And now?"

"Still is."

Determined to delay unpleasant thoughts as long as possible, Lottie insisted they clean up the kitchen when they finished eating.

She'd debated with herself about how much to tell Harve. Revealing what she suspected and accepting his assistance didn't mean she was going to hand control of her life over to him. She was in over her head and he was the logical one to help. Besides, he had a stake in this, too.

She wiped the countertops a second time, gathering and organizing her facts. Finally she decided she could delay no longer and went with him into the living room.

As she sank into an overstuffed chair opposite him, he handed her a glass of wine, from which she took a cautious sip. She needed to keep a clear head.

"Are you ready to discuss what happened this afternoon?" he asked. She noticed his voice was calm, not demanding, as if he was trying to avoid upsetting her.

She nodded.

"Then I guess my first question is, why did you tell Jeff the door was stuck? Why didn't you want him to know someone had deliberately locked you inside?"

"Because if he was the one who did it, he already knew, and if he wasn't, well...I guess I wanted time to get my thoughts together."

His eyebrows arched. "You really think Jeff locked you in there?"

"Yes. No. I don't know." She sighed. "I think I'd better tell you what's happened. Then you can ask questions. All right?"

"Any way you want to do it, Lottie."

She took a deep breath. "Okay," she said. "First of all I think someone's embezzling from the bank."

"What?" He shot to his feet. "Are you sure?"

"As much as I can be. I'm not an auditor. Or a criminal investigator. But that's what it looks like to me."

"How long have you known?"

She stared deliberately at the floor. "I suspected something was wrong two or three weeks ago, but I wasn't sure of what I was seeing. Then earlier this week I realized it might be embezzlement, but I still hoped I was wrong. Today, when I checked the records in the vault...well, I was sure. Or at least as sure as I can be. As I said, I'm no expert."

"Dammit, Lottie, why didn't you tell me?" She looked up to see him towering over her chair.

"Believe it or not, that's exactly what I was going to do. When I finished examining those old records, my first thought was to find you. That's...

that's when I discovered the door was stuck.''

She heard him take a sharp breath.

''Will you go sit down? You're standing too close. You make me nervous.''

''*I* make you nervous!''

''You know what I mean. Sit down, Harve,'' she ordered again, and this time he retreated to his chair.

''You should have told someone earlier,'' he said, his voice sounding patient and reasonable. ''What if I hadn't gone looking for you?''

''Then I would have spent more time locked in the vault,'' she said, and tried unsuccessfully to control a shiver. The expression on his face turned fierce.

''I couldn't tell anyone,'' she said, pleading for understanding, ''not until I had something more than an uneasy feeling or a slight suspicion. The last thing the bank needs now is another scandal. Particularly if there isn't grounds for one.''

''Okay,'' he granted. ''What convinced you? I'll try not to interrupt again.''

She took another sip of her wine, this time for courage. ''Do you recall a discussion about an investment account that was only paying about three percent interest? Abby said she complained about it at the board meeting.''

Harve nodded. ''I remember. I figured you'd switch that into treasury bonds as soon as you got your hands on it. They're paying at least six percent."

"I switched everything else," she told him, "but according to Uncle Cyrus, that particular account carries an early-withdrawal penalty and it matures in three months. The increased interest rate wouldn't have produced enough additional revenue to offset the withdrawal penalty between now and maturity. So I left it in place."

"Yes, I can see the sense in that."

"Well, that's the account that looks suspicious."

"I'm even less of an expert than you," he said. "Can you explain?"

She told him how, even though the figures balanced, something kept nagging at her when she'd examined the accounts, and how she'd finally realized the interest postings were the same from month to month.

"It didn't make sense, but I thought maybe the interest was paid at the end of a multimonth interest period, then retroactively posted as monthly amounts. I could only access the current year account from the computer in my office. Everything else is stored in the archives."

"If I understand you, you thought it might be an annual interest payment, that was recorded when earned rather than when received. Is that right?"

She nodded. "I've never seen an account set up like that, but I hoped... I wanted it to be true."

"Why didn't you ask someone?"

"I thought about it," she said, "but who should I have asked? I might have alerted exactly the wrong person."

He nodded, as if agreeing or at least accepting her reasoning. "That's when you decided to do a little detective work. Jeff was right to be suspicious of your clothing. You *planned* to go into the basement today."

"I thought it would be the perfect time," she said. "I would be alone, the bank closed. There wouldn't be anyone around to know what I was doing. It was daylight. No telltale lights burning to alert anyone I was working late."

"Obviously you miscalculated." She could hear the anger in his voice, but didn't think it was directed at her. "Someone knew."

"You're right," she agreed, "at least, partly right. No one could have known what I planned to do, but someone may have suspected I was investigating. Or just happened to discover me there and took advantage of the opportunity."

"Okay, let's go back to what you found."

"The same pattern of interest postings, the same amounts deposited to the investment account month after month after month."

"What does it mean?"

"It means someone may be reporting only part of the interest the account is earning and siphoning off the rest into another private account."

"In other words, embezzling?"

"In other words, embezzling," she echoed softly.

"How long has it been going on?" he asked.

"Five years."

"Five years?" He was on his feet again. "You think someone has been stealing bank funds for five years?"

"I said I wasn't sure," she protested. "And will you please sit down. You're making me—"

"I know, I know. I make you nervous. Someone can lock you in a bank vault and that's fine. Someone can sabotage your tire and that's all right. But I stand up and I make you nervous. All right. I'm sitting."

"What...what do you mean about my tire?" Her voice slid from surprise to anger. "You mean someone deliberately caused my flat?"

"I'm sorry, Lottie. I didn't mean to say that. I didn't want to frighten you, but yeah, I do think there's a possibility your flat wasn't chance. It could've been a freak accident, but after what you've just told me, I'm leaning toward deliberate act."

After a moment she confessed, "I thought it was a little strange, too, then decided I was imagining things. I guess we'll never know for sure."

"Probably not,"

"Okay, where was I?"

He grinned, one of those what-the-hell grins. "I was making you nervous."

It took her a moment to realize he was calling a time-out, a decompression break. And he was right, she needed it. He probably did, too.

"No," she told him. "Dizzy."

"What?"

"You weren't making me nervous. You were making me dizzy. All that walking back and forth, back and forth, back and forth—"

"Okay, okay. I get the picture. Would you like another glass of wine?"

This time she grinned back at him. "No, thank you. I'm fine."

He took a deep breath. "So what do we do now?"

"I'm not sure. That's one reason I was going to talk to you. I thought about contacting Chief Simpson, but I don't think he has authority here."

"I suspect you're right. The bank's under federal regulation. I'll get hold of my lawyer. He'll know. They'll probably start with an unscheduled audit by bank examiners and move on from there."

"It's going to be what Myrtle calls a bona fide scandal," Lottie said with a sigh.

"We don't have much choice."

"We don't have any choice at all," she corrected. "I know that."

"Do you have any idea who might be behind it, Lottie?"

She shook her head. "It could be anyone in the bank."

"What about Cyrus? You said he was the one who gave you the information on a penalty for early withdrawal. He must be familiar with the account."

"Technically he, Jefferson and yours truly are the only ones who have the authority to establish and manage the investment accounts," she said, "but in reality, everyone in the bank has access to the computer. Any of us could be manipulating the funds."

"If it's been going on for five years, that eliminates you."

"And probably Josephine Winters," Lottie said. "I think she's only been working for us for about four years."

"I'll call my lawyer tomorrow and—"

"Tomorrow's Sunday."

"With the retainer I pay him, he can work on Sunday. Anyway, I'll make the formal request for an audit. That'll keep some of the heat off you."

"It doesn't matter. I'm going to be right in the middle of it." She didn't want to mention her father, but there would be talk about him again, too. "The grapevine's going to be as busy as it was the time Preacher Riley ran off with Deacon Harlow's wife."

"I know. I'm sorry, Lottie."

She shrugged. "It can't be helped."

"There doesn't seem to be anything more we can do right now," Harve said. "Why don't we try the hot tub? I need to relax. I suspect you do, too."

The hot tub! In the past week she'd managed to push the memories of their dip in the hot tub to that place in the back of her mind that housed secret longings and remembered delights. The images came flooding back now, tantalizing and beckoning.

"If you're thinking about saying you should go home, it's not an option, Lottie," he warned. "Our embezzler has attacked you once, maybe twice, probably trying to distract you. The flat tire, if it wasn't an accident, was more annoying than threatening. Today's action was more dangerous. It's escalating. Until word is out that the embezzlement has been discovered, whoever it is may continue harassing you, hoping to keep you off balance, to keep you from looking at the records too closely. The next time you might get hurt."

She knew he was right. On all counts. Besides, she wanted to stay and her reason had nothing to do with threats or embezzlers. She wanted to stay here, with him. She also wanted him to realize it wasn't because he'd ordered her. Or coaxed her. She wasn't ready to examine her reasons too closely, only knew it was important for him to know she made her own decisions and was responsible for her own actions.

"I'll stay, as long as you realize you're risking your reputation," she said, keeping her voice light.

He cleared his throat. "If news that you stayed here tonight happened to get out, I suspect it would enhance, rather than damage, my reputation," he said. "But yours...I didn't think. Look, Lottie, I can take you to my grandmother's."

"And put her at risk? Absolutely not."

"Then I could ask her to play chaperon over here."

"Don't be ridiculous. My comment was a poor attempt at a joke. My reputation isn't at risk. Even if it was, it wouldn't matter. With this bank business, it's going to be dragged through the mud, anyway."

"No one will suspect you, Lottie."

"Ever hear the story about shooting the messenger?" At the look on his face she said, "Hey, I'm only kidding. Really. Besides, there's nothing either you or I can do about it. Now, did you mention the hot tub?"

HE WAS IN TROUBLE. Or to be perfectly honest, *still* in trouble. Harve stood in the darkness of his office staring out the window at a celestial light show as a spring storm front moved across the sky.

Upstairs, Lottie Carlyle was sleeping, peacefully he hoped, in one of the guest bedrooms. He was downstairs, in the middle of the night, pacing back and forth in the dark, trying to exhaust his body, if not his mind, enough to fall asleep, too.

He watched the giant forks of lightning playing peekaboo with the roiling dark clouds and idly observed that the storm would probably pass to the north of Little Falls.

He wanted Lottie, wanted her with an intensity that scared and surprised him. But there was more than hormones at work here. She was his emotional wellspring in an existence that, looking back, now seemed empty and desolate without her. When he was with her, the sun was brighter, the sky was bluer, the birdsong sweeter.

She was a private woman, focused, intelligent, confident of her abilities and determined to achieve her goals. A good match, he decided, for he recognized similar traits in himself. Two strong-willed people. One would not overwhelm the other.

She was courageous, too, almost to the point of foolhardiness. She challenged him and fascinated him and, at times, exasperated him.

During their discussion of the bank's current situation, he'd noted how carefully she'd avoided any mention of her father's crime and sensed she wasn't telling him everything. Was one connected to the other? Or were those memories simply too painful for her to share?

The storm was moving away, the lightning flashes less intense, the accompanying thunderclaps fainter, with longer intervals between light and sound.

He was determined not to rush her. Attempting to shoulder inherited responsibilities and liabilities, besieged by threats and suspicions, she didn't need the additional burden of dealing with his emotions. Or her own.

After a dip in the hot tub, she'd rejoined him in the living room. By unspoken agreement they'd avoided discussion of current and possible future unpleasantness, concentrating, instead, on memories of their childhoods—a happy innocent time where their lives had occasionally touched each other in the way lives in all small towns touch and connect.

The evening had passed quickly, almost too quickly. If he'd had the power, he would have prolonged it. He would have—

"Harve, is that you?"

Immersed in memories, he took a moment to return to the present. His body, however, responded to her voice immediately and accordingly. He turned and saw her standing in the doorway, silhouetted against the light from the hallway.

"Lottie? What are you doing down here? I thought you were asleep."

"I was for a while. I guess the thunder woke me up."

She stepped into the room, the embodiment of his most-longed-for fantasy. He flipped the light switch on the table lamp, a useless effort to cool the blood surging hotly through his veins.

She was wrapped in his terry-cloth robe, the sleeves rolled at the wrists, the hem stopping only inches above her ankles. She looked small and fragile, her dark hair sleep-tousled, her green eyes huge in the dim light.

"I was watching the storm. It looks like it missed us." Meaningless inconsequential conversation, he thought, designed to distract, to allow him to bolster his defenses.

It did neither.

She moved closer, until she was standing beside him by the window. "I always love watching storms. Sound and fury, light against darkness, all that unleashed power. Makes my problems seem puny."

"A visual demonstration that there are some things man can't control," he muttered.

"Who said *that?*"

"I did."

She grinned and leaned against his arm. "It sounded quite profound."

"Not pompous or pretentious?"

"No. Just truthful."

In the distance a spectacular fork of lightning lit the night sky. He settled his arm around her shoulders and pulled her into his side. Her soft voice floated upward. "...two potato, three potato, four potato..."

"What are you doing?"

"Counting seconds...five potato, six potato, seven potato, eight..."

The rumbling sound of thunder rolled over the house, strong enough to rattle the glass in the window.

"At least eight miles away," she said. "I think you're right. It's going to miss us."

"The speed of sound is 1,125 feet per second. That's about four seconds per mile."

"Now *that* sounded pompous," she told him, lifting her face toward him. The smile on her lips faded as his gaze caught hers.

"Lottie." He lowered his head, and their lips met in a kiss, sweet, gentle and full of promise. Desire coursed through him, thick as honey, hot as fire.

She made an inarticulate sound as her lips opened under his.

With a shudder that shook his body, he managed to raise his lips from hers. "I don't think we should be doing this," he said, his voice straining from the effort.

"I don't see why not. I'm going to be accused of it, anyway." She sighed and snuggled against him. "I want you," she said, her voice low and intense.

"Be sure, Lottie. Be very sure."

"I am."

He continued to hold her for a moment, common sense battling desire. Desire won. He swung her into his arms.

"What are you doing?"

"Taking you to bed."

## CHAPTER FOURTEEN

LOTTIE HID HER FACE in Harve's neck as he carried her down the hall to his bedroom. She felt the smooth silk of his robe beneath her cheek and wondered what, if anything, he wore beneath.

She was embarrassed by her boldness and encouraged by her success. She'd fallen in love with him; maybe she'd always been in love with him. Maybe he didn't love her; maybe his response was only a case of demanding hormones. Still, for tonight, at least she could pretend.

He lowered her gently onto a king-size bed and stretched out beside her, not touching, but close enough for her to feel the heat from his body.

In the dim light from a small lamp on the bedside table she could see the room was decorated in strong colors that seemed fitting for the man who slept here. The comforter was a surprise—large alternating stripes of warm soft velvet and cool sleek satin—rich, luxurious, seductive—and completely unexpected if one considered the generally accepted notion that for the past few years Harve had lived like a monk.

She raised her hand to touch his cheek, felt the

stubble of his beard. He sure didn't feel like a monk or look like a monk. His skin was warm to the touch and his eyes burned with a fire that threatened to bring her already heated blood to a boil.

"Do you know how long I've dreamed of your being here with me, of the two of us making love?" He turned his head to kiss her palm.

"How long?" she whispered.

"Too long. I want you, Lottie. I want you badly. If you're not sure, now is the time to say so, because I don't know how much longer I can be noble."

"Noble! Don't you dare. I seduced you. It's the first time I've ever tried to seduce anyone. And you...you want to be noble?"

He laughed then, a sound as much like a winner's trumpet as an expression of joy. "Believe me, I don't want to be noble." He captured her mouth in a searing kiss.

She matched him, heat with heat, fire with fire, her hands moving to push aside the lapels of his robe. Beneath the silk, his flesh was smooth and hot.

He gentled the kiss, nipping lightly at her lips. "Easy, love. We're in no hurry."

"I am," she all but gasped, desire flickering like flame along her nerves.

He laughed again, this time a low sound that rumbled from deep within his chest. "And I thought you were reserved."

"So did I. Harve—"

"Shh, love. Let me do this right." He rolled off the edge of the bed and slid to his feet in one continuous motion, untied his robe and let it fall to the floor.

He was magnificent, built long and lean, a study of planes and contours, his chest lightly furred, his arms and thighs muscular, his only covering cotton briefs. Plain white, she noticed, unpretentious and not designed to disguise his physical desire. Startled, she raised her eyes, only to have her gaze collide with his. His mouth spread into a grin as she felt heat rise in her cheeks.

"Your turn," he said softly, pulling her into a sitting position and peeling back the terry-cloth robe. "Like unwrapping a birthday present. Ah, perfect." He stood again, shed his briefs, then bent over her. With a featherlight touch, his fingers traced the spaghetti strap of her gown, then along the edge of the material to where it dipped between her breasts. He pushed her gently back against the pillows and followed her down.

She moved her hands over his shoulders, sliding them down his chest, feeling the beat of his heart under her touch, its racing rhythm a match for her own.

He replaced his fingers with his lips, his mouth tracing the same path downward. Then with a low growl, he nuzzled the material of her gown aside and took her nipple into his mouth.

Fireworks, skyrockets, the Fourth of July—she arched upward, her arms wrapping around his neck, pulling him closer as wave after wave of sensation swept over her. He sought her other nipple, repeating the splendid torture.

"Harve," she gasped.

He moved his mouth upward. "Can you feel how much I want you?" he whispered against her lips. He lifted the hem of her gown, helped her pull it over her head, then dropped it to the floor.

She reached for him again, wanting him close, marveling in the feel of his bare skin against hers. His hands skimmed her waist, her hips, the friction of his touch sweet torture. When he found her mouth, his kiss was warm and sweet, then hot and demanding.

"Tell me what you **wa**nt," he whispered.

"You, Harve. I want you."

She heard herself protest as he rolled away for a moment, reaching for the packet she didn't realize he'd laid on the bedside table. Then he was back.

"And I want you."

He settled himself between her thighs and entered her slowly, as if savoring each moment. When he began to move within her, she twisted wildly, meeting each thrust eagerly. And when eventually she felt him shudder and heard him call her name, she dissolved in a series of mind-shattering explosions.

HARVE LAY in the darkness, Lottie sleeping beside him, sweet and soft and infinitely precious. He wanted to stay like this forever, holding her, loving her, protecting her. Did she know what she did to him, how she affected him? She was in his blood, so essentially a part of him he couldn't imagine how he'd survived all these years without her.

They'd made love again, slowly, savoring each touch, each taste. She was like wild honey, he thought—smooth and natural and incredibly sweet.

He turned onto his side, cradling her in his arms, closed his eyes and soon joined her in sleep.

THE RING OF THE PHONE, loud and persistent, jerked him from sleep. Fumbling in the dark, he grabbed for the receiver, his heart pounding as he recognized the almost certain urgency inherent in a middle-of-the-night call. He felt Lottie stir beside him.

It was his grandmother on the other end of the line.

"Thank goodness, you're home!" Her voice was frantic. "Lottie's house is on fire! Her car's in the garage, but they can't find—"

"It's all right, Grandmother. Lottie's not home. She's fine. She's here with me."

He heard Lottie gasp.

From his grandmother there was a small startled sound, a moment of silence, an indrawn breath and then, "She's with you? I mean…well, thank goodness—"

"I'll explain later. I'll call you back," he said quickly. He hung up the phone, switched on the bedside lamp, then turned to Lottie. The accusation in her eyes made him flinch.

"Your grandmother! Did you have to tell your grandmother that we...that I...?"

He reached for her, ignoring her struggles and pulled her into his arms. "Easy, love. I had to. She was in a panic."

He held her close, wishing there was some other way to tell her. "Grandmother says your house is on fire."

LOTTIE COULD SMELL smoke and the charred wet wood as they approached her house. She leaned forward, expecting the worst, and released a long breath when she saw, in the glare of the volunteer fire department's portable floodlights, the structure still standing. Whatever the damage, it wasn't apparent from the front of the house.

Harve drove the truck onto the lawn, presumably to keep the driveway clear for fire-department equipment. As he walked beside her toward the back of house, he took her hand in his and gave it a comforting squeeze.

When they rounded the corner of the house, she could see that most of the damage was confined to the back porch and kitchen area. Store owner Isaac Easton, who served as Little Falls's volunteer fire chief, was standing to one side of what used to be the porch, writing in a small notepad.

Another fireman played a stream of water over a pile of smoldering debris, which had apparently been removed from the house. Little, if anything, in the heap, was identifiable. He looked up as they approached, and it took Lottie a moment to recognize Clyde Ashton with his soot-blackened face.

"Hey, Chief," he called. "Here's Ms. Carlyle."

Chief Easton shoved the notepad into his back pocket and hurried toward them. "Sure glad to see you, Ms. Carlyle. For a while there we were worried you were inside."

"I'm sorry," she said. "I hope no one was hurt...."

"Nope. Everybody's fine. We did have to break down your front door, though. We couldn't get in through the back because of the fire. But don't you worry, I'll board it up before we leave."

"What happened, Isaac?" Harve asked.

"Don't rightly know," the chief replied. He turned to Lottie. "You had painting and cleaning supplies stored on the back porch, didn't you?"

She nodded mutely.

"Near as I can tell, that's where it started. It looks worse than it is, Ms. Carlyle. Most of the fire damage is confined to the back porch and the porch-kitchen common wall. There's smoke throughout the house of course and maybe some water damage in the kitchen and back hall. That's one first-class fire alarm you installed. Woke up half the neighborhood. Three of them called in, even old Jack Bailey. He said it sounded like London during the blitz. I don't know if he was really there or not, in London, I mean, but he's old enough. Half-deaf, too. Like I said, a good alarm."

"But the fire's out now? I mean, is it safe for me to go inside?"

"Oh, it's out all right. Clyde's just wetting down that pile of stuff we pulled off the porch, in case there's a spark or two left. But I don't know if I'd go wandering around in there just yet. There's still a lot of smoke. And it's dark. We had to cut off the electricity until we can access the damage. Yep, all in all, I'd say we were real lucky. Good thing those cleaning rags smoldered so long, too. I figure that's what set off the alarm. The fire was just really starting when we got here."

"Rags? What rags? There weren't any rags on the back porch," she protested.

"You said you had cleaning supplies out there, Ms. Carlyle."

"Supplies, yes, cleaners, some water-based paint, but nothing flammable. And no rags. I'm very careful about things like that and so is the contractor who's working here," she said. "I didn't leave any rags on the back porch, Chief Easton. I'm absolutely positive."

Harve put a hand on her shoulder. "Are you sure there were rags, Isaac?"

"Hell, yes, I'm sure. Like I said, some of them were still smoldering when we got here. Come to think of it, we've probably got parts of them in that heap of wet debris over there. First thing we did was rake all that junk off the porch."

Harve took a step toward the pile.

"You hold it right there, Harve. Don't go messing in things when you don't know what you're doing. I'll be calling the county fire marshal. He handles suspected arson cases."

"You think it was arson?" Lottie gasped. "Someone deliberately set my house on fire?"

"I'm no expert, Ms. Carlyle, but if you didn't leave those rags on the porch, someone else put them there. I don't want you going into the house, either. Not until the marshal's been here. He'll probably want to talk to you tomorrow, too. You got a place to stay?"

"She'll be at the farm," Harve told him.

"Ms. Abigail's or your place?" Isaac asked. The question seemed innocent enough, but Lottie thought she heard a certain innuendo in his voice.

"She'll be at my place," Harve said, his voice firm and rather cold. "From what you're telling us, someone may have deliberately set Ms. Carlyle's house on fire. There's no reason to suspect they didn't believe she was asleep inside. Nor is there any reason to believe they might not try to harm her again. I will not put my grandmother at risk. Ms. Carlyle will be safer at my place. If anyone wants to harm her, they're going to have to go through me first."

"I understand," the chief said perhaps a little meekly.

"You will, of course, let the fire marshal know where she is?" Harve added.

"Yes. Yes, I certainly will. I think that's a good idea, Harve. She'll be safer with you."

"Good. Then if there's nothing more we can do here, we may as well leave. Good night, Chief."

"Night, Harve, Ms. Carlyle."

"Good night, Chief Easton," Lottie said softly. "Thank you and the rest of the volunteers for your help."

"Glad to do it, ma'am. I'm glad, too, it wasn't any worse. This is a grand old house."

"He was trying to get back in your good graces," Lottie whispered to Harve as they walked back toward the truck.

"And yours," Harve said. "Good thing, too." His voice was almost a growl.

"He wasn't thinking anything the rest of the town won't think when they find out I'm staying with you," she told him.

"Ah, but we've given them a reasonable excuse, one they can and probably will accept," he said. "It also happens to be true. I want you where I know you'll be safe until this is over. I'll get Grandmother or Annie to act as chaperon, if it'll make you feel better."

"No, that's not necessary," she said. "I want to stay with you. If the town is scandalized, tough."

"They're gossiping busybodies," he said, "but for the most part, they're not malicious."

"I know." She actually managed a smile. "Why watch soap operas on television when you can be part of the cast?"

By the time they arrived back at the farm, the eastern horizon was turning from gray to pink. At Harve's insistence, Lottie went back to bed, even though she was sure she'd be unable to sleep.

She was surprised and disoriented when he woke her several hours later.

"Adrenaline letdown," he told her. "The body will stand only so much, then it insists on shutting down, taking a rest. Yesterday was a busy day. First you discover what looks like bank theft, then you find yourself locked in a bank vault. Finally someone sets your house on fire."

*And we also made love,* Lottie thought. *Maybe it was nothing unusual for you, but for me...it was extraordinary.*

*And wonderful.*

"You needed the rest," Harve continued. "I would have let you sleep longer, but the fire marshal called to say he was on his way out here. I thought you'd want a few minutes to get dressed. Breakfast in the kitchen when you're ready."

She was sitting at the kitchen table sipping a cup

of coffee when Fred Madison, the county fire marshal, arrived. Harve led him into the kitchen.

He was slightly rotund with thinning salt-and-pepper hair. His summer suit was wrinkled, and the knot of his tie had slipped half an inch down from the top of his collar opening. He reminded her of the proverbial absentminded professor—until she looked into his eyes. A deep brown, they were sharp and assessing. This man, she thought, is not as innocuous or benign as he appears.

"Why don't you sit down, Mr. Madison," Harve suggested, "and I'll pour you a cup of coffee. Or something else? Water? Orange juice?"

"Coffee would be fine," he said, sitting in a chair directly opposite Lottie. He immediately got down to business. "I understand from Chief Easton that you claim you stored no dirty cleaning rags on the back porch," he said, his voice neither accusing nor questioning.

"That's right, Mr. Madison."

"You're having some construction work done. Would the contractor or any of his helpers have left anything like that lying around?"

"No," she said. "Both the contractor and I are very careful. The house is wood frame and over 150 years old. The wood's tinder dry. The contractor only recently completed the scraping and repainting on the back side of the house. He recommended we use a fire retardant under the oil-based paint he's using on the exterior. Said the oil paint is more volatile and harder to use than water-based acrylics, but it gives the old wood better protection from the elements. He insisted the unused paint not be stored in or around the house. So it's in a small gardening shed out back.

"I'm very careful about potential fire hazards, Mr. Madison. There was nothing on the back porch but several cans of water-based paint being used inside the house, some wallpaper paste and various cleaning detergents. Nothing flammable and absolutely no rags, dirty or clean."

He looked at her sharply. "You say there was a fire-retardant solution recently applied to the wood under the fresh paint?"

She nodded.

"That probably explains why the fire didn't catch hold more quickly. Such old wood—I'd have expected it to go up like a torch."

He paused a moment, idly drumming his fingers on the tabletop. "I had a good look at the scene this morning, Ms. Carlyle, and I can tell you that the source of the fire was unquestionably dirty rags. It could have been spontaneous combustion, or something else could have set it off. Thanks to Chief Easton's quick thinking in raking everything movable off that back porch and hosing it down, we were able to recover some remnants. Lab tests should be able to identify the solutions on them.

"I don't believe it'll be gasoline or anything extremely volatile," he added. "The fire took hold too slowly. I'm expecting some everyday household solution, like furniture polish. It'd cause the rags to burn more readily, but not explosively, if you know what I mean. Careless disposal of cleaning items is a major cause of household fires.''

"I'm aware of that," Lottie told him. "And I'll tell you again, I didn't leave dirty cleaning rags lying around."

The fire marshal held up his hand. "I believe you, Ms. Carlyle. I'll admit, when I came out here, I expected to discover you'd been careless. But after talking with you, I'm convinced otherwise. Which leaves us with the very probable chance that the fire was intentionally set. It was either an amateur effort, someone using what they had at hand, or, and I think this more likely, someone wanting it to look like a careless accident if the source was discovered. Do you have any enemies, Ms. Carlyle? Have you recently been threatened in any way?''

The suddenness of his questions startled her. She looked helplessly at Harve.

"He's a professional law-enforcement official, Lottie. Spreading rumors would be as detrimental to his investigation as to ours. I think we're going to have to tell him everything. It may all tie together.''

Madison looked from one to the other. "What's going on here? Perhaps you should explain....''

Lottie took a deep breath and when Harve gave her an encouraging nod, she started talking. She told him about her suspicions, about her Saturday-afternoon investigation into the archives, about the door not opening when she tried to leave.

Then Harve took over, explaining how, when he couldn't find her, he contacted a bank official to search the premises. "She'd been deliberately locked in," Harve told him. "I took the bolt out of the hasp myself."

"Who else knows this?" Madison asked.

"No one, except the person who did it. Jeff—Jefferson Blackburn, the bank's other vice president—was with me, but he was searching upstairs when I heard her pounding on the door from inside the vault. By the time he joined us, I'd removed the bolt and she was free. She told him that the door had stuck. I didn't tell him differently."

"Why did you do that?"

"I didn't want anyone asking questions until we could call in the bank examiners," Lottie explained.

"There's also another incident, or at least a possible incident," Harve said. "A couple of weeks ago Lottie had a flat tire that left her stranded on the road after dark. It may have been an accident, but I don't like the coincidence. The tire had been punctured with a sharp instrument in the sidewall, very near the wheel rim. And one of the lug nuts was mangled so badly the flat couldn't be changed. The service station had to cut the lug nut off and rethread the bolt."

The fire marshal stared at the table for a moment

as if collecting his thoughts. Then he picked up the coffee cup, took a sip and carefully returned it to the saucer. "At this point, Ms. Carlyle," he said, looking at her, "I have to say it sounds like you have a real enemy. Has anything else happened, anything at all, that might be considered threatening?"

His direct question again caught Lottie by surprise. *The notes.* She made a small sound of distress. *Heaven help me, Harve is going to be furious I didn't tell him about the notes.*

"Besides a mysterious flat tire, being locked in a vault and having her house set on fire, you mean?" Harve demanded. "Isn't that enough?" Harve demanded.

But the fire marshal had seen her reaction. "Ms. Carlyle?" he said quietly.

"With everything happening, I forgot them." She gave Harve a pleading look. "I didn't think they were important and then I forgot. Honest."

"Forgot what, Ms. Carlyle?" Madison asked.

"The note—notes," she said.

"What notes?" Harve sounded incredulous.

"I found a note on my desk at the bank saying I wasn't welcome in Little Falls. I didn't know who sent it and figured there was no way of finding out, so I—"

"Didn't think they were important? You have a suspicious flat tire on the road at night. You get locked in a bank vault and could have been there most of the weekend. Then your house is set on fire. And you don't think an anonymous note is important?'' Although Harve's voice was low when he started speaking, by the time he finished, it was nearly a shout.

"When you put it like that, it sounds pretty stupid,'' she conceded, "but when I found the note, nothing had happened yet.''

"You said notes,'' Madison interjected. "Was there more than one?''

She nodded. "There was a second one a couple of weeks later.''

"And you didn't think to mention it, either?'' Although spoken more softly, Harve's voice still had the intensity of a shout.

"Mr. Tremayne, I agree that under the circumstances it doesn't seem wise for Ms. Carlyle not to have mentioned them,'' Madison said calmly, "but she does not appear to be a foolish woman. Now, why don't we listen to her explanation?''

At least the fire marshal was willing to be reasonable, Lottie thought. "Thank you,'' she said, giving him a smile. "The first note was on my desk the first day I went to work at the bank. I had no idea who might have left it there. Everyone in the bank and half the community had been in my office that day. I saw no reason to make it public. It would only have caused talk, and the bank didn't need that kind of publicity. When nothing else happened after several weeks, I simply put it out of my mind.''

"And the second one?" Harve asked.

"I found it the Monday after my flat tire, but I hadn't cleaned off my desk in a week. It could have been there one day or six days before I found it. I didn't realize there *was* anything suspicious about the flat tire," she added, looking directly at Harve. "You didn't tell me."

He acknowledged her accusation with a curt nod.

"Anyway, my reasons for not going public were the same. I didn't believe an anonymous note was a real threat, and the bank didn't need the bad publicity."

"That sounds like a logical explanation to me, even if perhaps not the wisest," Madison said. "Do you still have the notes?"

"Yes. I stuck them in my briefcase, intending to throw them away."

"Your briefcase is in the living room," Harve said. "I'll get it."

When he returned with it, Lottie reached inside and handed the fire marshal the two envelopes. Madison carefully removed and unfolded the notes. Harve's face turned white as he read them over the marshal's shoulder.

Lottie had no desire to look at them again. The words were burned into her mind, especially in light of recent events.

"No one's touched them but you?" Madison asked.

"And now you," Lottie said.

"Then we may as well try to preserve them for possible evidence," he said, and asked Harve if he had a clean plastic bag.

When Harve got one from a kitchen drawer, the fire marshal slipped the notes inside. "You were wrong about one aspect, Ms. Carlyle," he said turning to Lottie. "In addition to the possibility of fingerprints, if it becomes necessary, the experts can discover quite a bit of information about the note sender. They should be able to determine which publications the note material was cut from, maybe even which issues of those publications. They might even be able to determine who, among their major suspects, regularly reads or subscribes to those particular publications."

"How on earth could they do that?"

Madison shrugged. "Identifying the publications is a matter of matching typefaces and analyzing paper content. And most magazines and newspapers sell their subscriber lists. If not, in the case of a particular suspect, they could request that the publisher furnish us with the information, either voluntarily or under court order."

"You mean, if I'd reported the notes, they could have discovered who sent them?"

"No, not at all," Madison explained. "At the time and without any evidence of violence, they would have been considered simple harassment. Irritating, but not dangerous. That, however, is no longer the case."

"In other words they have now become important," Harve said.

"May have become important, depending on what other evidence we find or don't find," Madison said. "Such an investigation would be expensive and time-consuming. It would only be undertaken if other evidence isn't available."

He turned to Lottie. "I think we all agree the notes no longer seem at all benign. Someone indeed means you harm."

"I'll be keeping a close eye on her," Harve said.

Madison nodded. "What are you doing about the suspected embezzlement?"

"I've contacted my lawyer," Harve said. "He'll be notifying bank examiners first thing in the morning. I expect them on the scene by Tuesday."

"Recontact him, tell him about the fire and have him pass my name on to authorities," the fire marshal said. "I'll coordinate with them when they contact me. Meanwhile we'll get those rag remnants into the laboratory and see what information they can give us.

"And you, Ms. Carlyle," he said, turning to look at her, "you be very, very careful."

## CHAPTER FIFTEEN

AFTER OBTAINING the fire marshal's permission, Harve went with Lottie to her house Sunday afternoon to survey the damage and retrieve some of her clothes.

Chief Easton had been as good as his word, securing the broken front door and boarding up entry to the rest of the house from the fire-damaged area. Lottie was relieved when a daylight inspection of the kitchen proved the chief had been correct when he'd said most of the damage was confined to the common wall of the porch and kitchen.

"The kitchen cabinets aren't damaged," Harve assured her after carefully examining the chestnut wood for scorching. "They only need to be cleaned and polished again."

Harve helped her make a list of necessary repairs. A portion of the new kitchen tile would have to be replaced, as would the kitchen wallpaper. Considering the potential for damage, Lottie knew she'd been lucky.

Everything in her closet smelled of smoke. She carefully selected several washable outfits to take to the farm and laid aside others to drop off at the dry cleaners on Monday.

She also, over Harve's protests, got her car from the garage. Although she'd agreed to stay with him at the farm, she was determined to be as discreet as possible.

"I'm not going to flaunt the fact that I'm staying with you," she told him. "I'll drive my own car back and forth to work."

Under the circumstances, however, she didn't argue about his declared intention to keep a close watch over her. The incidents of the past two days had left her truly shaken.

HARVE FOLLOWED HER into town Monday morning, traveling only a few car lengths behind her, even parking in front of the bank until he'd seen her enter safely.

He made her promise not to leave town this afternoon until he was on hand to follow her back out to the farm.

Lottie entered the bank tense and nervous and doing her best to hide it. The normal business-as-usual atmosphere seemed almost unreal; of course, she was the only one who knew bank examiners would soon be swooping down on them. She wondered if anyone would give himself away when they arrived?

Everyone in the bank seemed to know of her Saturday adventure in the basement vault. Obviously Jeff had spread the news.

"Can't imagine why you'd want to go poking around downstairs," her uncle said gruffly. "Still, I'm glad Jeff found you."

"It's an old building, Uncle Cyrus. Old doors often stick," she told him, trying to pass it off as an accident. She smiled at Jeff. "But I'm grateful for the rescue, too."

"It won't happen again," her cousin said. "I'm having a phone installed in the vault this morning."

Good idea if being stuck in the vault was an accident, Lottie knew, but whoever had locked her inside wouldn't hesitate to cut a phone line first. She shivered.

Her adventure in the locked vault was not common knowledge outside the bank, but her house fire was community news. Customers made it a point to tell her how sorry they were about the fire and to express hope the damage wasn't extensive. They seemed to believe it was an accident, too, and she didn't tell them differently.

Instead of eating lunch in her office, her normal practice, she left the bank and walked down the street to the Down Home. Chatting with Myrtle was always a comfort.

Not today, however. "First you get stuck in the basement bank vault," Myrtle began, "then your house nearly burns down. Are you going to tell me what's going on?"

Lottie wondered how Myrtle had learned about the bank-vault incident, but she didn't bother to ask. She knew Myrtle wouldn't tell her.

"It isn't as bad as it sounds," Lottie said. "The vault was a little scary, but I wasn't in any danger. And I wasn't at home when the house caught on fire."

"Sounds to me like you need a keeper."

Lottie couldn't control the furious color that stained her cheeks.

"Aha," Myrtle said teasingly. "So maybe you've found one? Maybe a nice tall handsome horse rancher?"

"Don't be ridiculous, Myrtle." Lottie blushed even more. "Harve's a friend. He's helping me. That's all."

"If you say so, but I still think it's a shame the two of you don't get together."

"Myrtle..." Lottie pleaded.

"Oh, all right. I'll wait until you're ready to tell me. But do one thing for me now. Promise you'll be careful. There's something going on—something more than what's between you and a certain handsome cowboy, I mean. I don't like the feelings I'm getting. Not at all. And you tell that keeper of yours I said for him to be careful, too, you hear?"

No, Lottie acknowledged as she walked back to the bank, her visit with Myrtle certainly hadn't made her feel any better.

Although Harve had told her it would probably

take at least twenty-four hours to get the auditing team together, she was on pins and needles most of the afternoon, unable to decide which was worse—anticipating their arrival or dreading it.

Nothing but her own thoughts, however, broke the normal routine of the day. She left the bank only minutes after the three-thirty closing time. No staying late alone today. Or in the foreseeable future, she decided. She'd arrive and leave on time until this was over.

She immediately saw Harve waiting in his truck across the street from where she'd parked her car. He pushed his Stetson back from his forehead, signaling he'd seen her, then started the truck. By the time she pulled out of her parking spot, he was ready to fall into place behind her.

At any other time she would have found his protectiveness irritating, maybe even smothering. But not now. Every time she glanced in her rearview mirror and saw the big green pickup, all she felt was gratitude.

She wondered how long it would take someone in town to figure out he was doing guard duty. Not long, she decided. Probably no later than tomorrow. But by then the whole town would probably know about the trouble at the bank. They'd have something else to talk about.

Lord, but she wished it was over. Trying to act normal as she waited for the examiners to put in an appearance was proving more difficult than she'd imagined.

Both Abby and Annie had been told the circumstances—about the locked vault door and the suspected arson—to justify her reason for staying with Harve, instead of in the apartment at Abigail's.

Abby took exception to the idea that she couldn't protect herself and Lottie.

"Let me get my shotgun and I'll take care of anybody who comes around here with mischief in mind," she insisted, but had finally agreed that Harve would serve as a more efficient deterrent, shotgun or not.

When Lottie and Harve arrived at the farm, Annie was in the process of fixing dinner, including one of her famous blackberry pies. Lottie knew it was the housekeeper's way of saying she approved, or at least didn't disapprove, of Lottie's temporary move to the farm.

Annie had also laundered Lottie's smoke-scented clothes and hung them conspicuously in one of the upstairs guest rooms. Another hint, Lottie thought. This one said, *Behave yourself.*

When Annie left, Harve played the part of attentive host, kind, considerate and concerned, but with never a suggestion or reference to the intimacy they'd shared two nights ago.

*Was his lovemaking only a matter of galloping hormones, after all?*

Frustrated and miserable, Lottie finally excused

herself to go upstairs. *I can't even look forward to feeling better tomorrow....*

HARVE WATCHED Lottie walk up the stairs. Alone. It was the hardest thing he'd ever done.

He wanted to take her in his arms and soothe away the hurt and misery he saw in her eyes. He wanted to help her forget her worries about the bank, the threats, the uncertainty. He wanted to hold her close, to assure her everything would be all right.

He didn't dare touch her.

One touch and his carefully forged control would vanish like smoke. He'd wanted to make love to her so completely she forgot everything else. He'd have her in his bed every night, their bodies and lives intertwined, as lovers and partners.

That couldn't happen yet. He had demanded she stay with him at the farm for other reasons. She was hurt, confused and vulnerable. He wouldn't, couldn't take advantage of the circumstances or her. Their personal relationship had to be put on hold until this was over, until the embezzler was unmasked and she was safe. Until then he'd guard her and protect her, but she'd sleep upstairs in her bed and he'd toss and turn downstairs in his.

He was a patient man, at least he'd always considered himself a patient man, but some things even a patient man shouldn't be asked to endure. *Please God, let this be over soon.*

TUESDAY DAWNED bright and warm for mid-June. The temperature was already in the midseventies and rising as Lottie, driving her car and closely followed by Harve in the truck, left the farm for downtown.

Once again Harve admonished her to wait for him that afternoon before driving back out to the farm.

The bank examiners arrived at nine-forty-five, flashing credentials and demanding admittance. Carrying calculators and laptop computers, they took over the boardroom and began the auditing process.

Although they were behind closed doors, out of the public's sight, no one in the bank could ignore or forget their presence. The atmosphere was tense and anxious.

Not surprising, Lottie thought, for it was, after all, normal to be worried and concerned about what was happening around you; it didn't mean you were guilty. Heck, *she* was worried and she knew she wasn't guilty. Besides, everyone in the bank couldn't be guilty, could they?

Jeff stalked into her office at midmorning. "It was you," he accused. "You called in the examiners, didn't you? That's what you were doing in the vault Saturday. Darn it, Lottie, if you had questions, why didn't you come and ask me? Or my father? This is going to tear the bank apart."

Lottie wanted to believe his protest was innocent,

his outrage righteous. But someone was guilty. It could be him.

"You really believe they're going to find something wrong, don't you?" he went on, his tone horrified now.

*He's either innocent or a darn good actor,* she thought.

"That's right, isn't it?" he demanded again. "You think something's wrong."

She thought about pretending ignorance. After all, he couldn't know for sure she was the one who'd alerted authorities. Then she decided it didn't matter. Not anymore. "I did what I had to do," she told him. "And yes, Jeff, I do think something's very wrong."

She stayed in her office during the lunch hour, not wanting to face the buzz of speculation she was afraid was sweeping down Main Street. Although the examiners' arrival had been fairly inconspicuous, she was pretty certain their presence would soon be known. No secret could escape the attention of the town's well-developed grapevine for long.

As the afternoon wore on, the atmosphere in the bank became more oppressive, the temperature outside hotter. What began as an warm morning was turning into an unbearably hot day, with more such days expected, according to the weather forecaster. She didn't understand the explanations about wind currents and weather fronts and stalled highs, but it didn't take a rocket scientist to see the mercury on the outdoor thermometer was registering in the mid-nineties.

When the banking day finally ended, she was more than ready to leave. One of the other bank officials, probably Jeff, would have to stay on the premises while the examiners continued to work. She wasn't about to volunteer.

Harve was again waiting for her across the street. When they arrived at the farm, he told her he'd started filling the swimming pool earlier in the day and thought they should be able to take a dip later in the evening. Annie said she'd fixed a cold dinner because it was too hot to cook.

"Hasn't been this hot this early since 1963," she muttered. Apparently Annie hadn't yet heard about the bank examiners, but Lottie knew the house-keeper would have caught up on the gossip by the time she saw her again tomorrow, and then the questions would begin. Like everyone else in town, Annie would want to know what was going on.

The evening passed much like the previous evening with Harve acting kind and supportive, but aloof. Even during their swim in the pool, he seemed reserved. She was glad to escape upstairs to her bedroom.

Wednesday at the bank was even worse than Tuesday.

Somehow Josephine kept a determined smile on her face as she waited on customers, but the strain she no doubt felt was evident. Of all the bank employees, she was the only one Lottie could eliminate as a suspect because Josephine hadn't been working at the bank five years ago.

Jeff wandered around looking anxious and distressed, avoiding Lottie as much as possible.

Cyrus floated in and out of his office, his complexion even paler than usual. Shortly before noon, Emma buzzed Lottie on the intercom. "Mr. Blackburn would like to see you in his office," she announced, her voice frosty.

"I'll be right there," Lottie told her, somewhat surprised by the summons. She'd thought Cyrus would try to pretend nothing was wrong.

"Even though I was against your coming into the bank, I didn't believe you would deliberately try to destroy it," her uncle said as soon as she entered his office. "You're William Carlyle's daughter, but you're also a Blackburn. I foolishly believed you had some family loyalty."

"This isn't about family loyalty, Uncle Cyrus," Lottie said. "I had no choice. I discovered a problem in the books and notified authorities. I would like to think that, had it been you, you'd have done the same thing."

"There's nothing wrong with the books," he protested.

"Then we have nothing to worry about, have we?"

"Once this fiasco is over, the board will demand your resignation," he warned.

Was his outrage genuine, she wondered, or was he bluffing? "I guess we'll have to wait and see," she murmured.

Emma also managed to voice her disapproval as Lottie left her uncle's office. "You should be ashamed causing all this upset," the secretary said.

Even Hiram's usually stoic demeanor slipped after he carried several ledgers into the boardroom for the examiners. The bookkeeper seemed extremely rattled. Shortly after noon he reported he wasn't feeling well and went home. Josephine told Lottie it was the first time she could remember Hiram's requesting sick leave since she'd started work at the bank.

After work Harve followed Lottie to her house. She wanted to see how the repair work was progressing. She also wanted to check the rose garden, worried that with the high heat, the plants might need additional water.

"Hey, Ms. Carlyle, there's a kid out back looking for you," one of the construction workers called to her as she drove up.

Probably Gayle, Lottie thought, afraid she knew why Jeff's daughter was looking for her. She found the girl in the rose garden.

"I won't be coming over anymore," Gayle told her. "I only came to water today because it was so hot, but I'm not coming back."

"All right," Lottie said thoughtfully. "Well, thank you for letting me know. And thank you for all your help. I really appreciate it. I'll miss you."

Gayle didn't reply. She turned around and, dragging the hose, walked several feet deeper into the garden. Although the child hadn't mentioned it, Lottie was sure the situation at the bank had something to do with why Gayle wouldn't be caring for the garden any longer.

Lottie hesitated. She wanted to say something more, wanted to assure Gayle that everything would turn out all right, but she didn't know how to approach the subject. Besides, she wasn't sure everything *would* be all right where the girl was concerned. For chances were good that either Gayle's father or her grandfather was about to be exposed as an embezzler. Maybe worse.

Had Jeff forbidden his daughter to help Lottie with the roses?

Lottie was still debating what to say when Gayle whirled back around to face her. "My daddy didn't steal from the bank," she said, her voice quavering. "You shouldn't have said that. He wouldn't steal from anyone."

"Did your father tell you I accused him of stealing?" Lottie asked carefully.

Gayle shook her head, tears coursing down her cheeks.

"He didn't tell me anything. Nobody tells me

anything," she sobbed, "but I heard him and Mom talking. You shouldn't have said he was stealing."

"I didn't," Lottie said, moving closer to the girl. "I did find what looks like some errors in the bank books and according to the law, I'm required to call authorities to audit the records. If your father had found the same errors, he would have done the same thing."

Lottie wasn't certain her explanation was getting through to Gayle. More firmly she went on, "I never said your father was stealing. I never said *anyone* was stealing. I'm not going to lie to you. That's what *might* have happened, but it also might be nothing more than mistakes in the record keeping. The authorities will decide whether it's theft or a mistake when they finish the audit. And if the records show someone has been stealing, they'll investigate to find out who it is. Until then, no one is accused of stealing. Not your father. Not anyone."

She paused. "I think you should talk to your father and mother about what you overheard, honey, because I suspect you didn't hear the entire conversation. If you want to, you can tell them what I told you and that I suggested you talk to them about it. But don't expect your father to have all the answers, Gayle. Right now no one knows what the problem is, only that there *is* a problem. Okay?"

"Okay," the girl agreed, "but I'm still not coming back."

"I understand," Lottie told her, reaching for the

hose. "I'll finish the watering. You go talk to your folks."

Harve stepped around the hedge moments after Gayle disappeared. "I heard the two of you talking," he said. "I didn't want to interrupt."

"That was probably best." Lottie nodded. "She's very upset. Did you hear the conversation?"

"Most of it."

"Did I...should I have said something else? Or have told her something different?"

"No, I don't think so. You told her the truth as far as you could. All you really know. I think that's always the best. You identify with her, don't you?"

Lottie nodded again. "I remember not believing...not wanting to believe my father was guilty. What if Jeff turns out to be— Oh, Harve, she's so young. Younger even than I was."

"Don't borrow trouble, Lottie. Remember, whatever happens, you're not at fault. Even if Jeff turns out to be the guilty one, I suspect Gayle and Jeannie won't be made the pariahs you and your mother were. You won't let that happen. Neither will I."

By the next day it was obvious the news that "something's going on at the bank" was circulating on the street. Foot traffic at the bank was heavier than usual for a midweek, midmonth day, with customers inventing reasons for stopping by.

Charlie Zimmermann brought in thirty-five dollars to deposit to the barbershop account. Jacob Calley came in to place an order for checks embossed with the feed store's name, then claimed he'd forgotten he'd ordered five hundred just the week before. Even Billy Bob Simpson, his police-chief badge brightly polished on his uniform shirt, stopped by "just to see if everything's all right."

Lottie had no way of knowing how much of the talk on the street was actual information and how much was speculation, but she suspected she wasn't the only bank employee lying low. She wished she could talk to Myrtle, but lacked the courage to go to the Down Home. Neither Myrtle nor the town's residents would be shy about asking questions and she didn't have the answers. The bank examiners remained isolated behind closed doors as they continued to study records.

Outside the heat wave continued.

That afternoon, when she and Harve arrived back at the farm, they saw an unfamiliar vehicle parked by the house.

"It's an investigator," Harve told her before they went inside. "He wants to talk to you—but outside the bank."

"How did he find out I was staying here?"

"I suspect he contacted my attorney. Or maybe they talked to the fire marshal."

"Do you think this means they've found something?"

"It sounds like it," Harve said, "but I didn't get that from the investigator. He's pretty close-mouthed. Just showed me his credentials and asked if he could come and speak with you here. That's all."

The man was waiting in the living room. He introduced himself as Federal Investigator Martin Ludlow and showed her his identification.

"FBI?" she asked.

"Not exactly, although we may well be coordinating with them before this is over," he said. "Crimes against banks fall under federal jurisdiction because banks are regulated under federal law. By extension crimes against persons threatened or harmed because they are engaged in the performance of their duties within a federally regulated institution can also fall within the providence of federal authority."

Lottie caught herself smiling and covered it with a little cough. She'd never accuse Harve of being pompous again. Whatever else he was, she'd bet Mr. Ludlow was also an attorney. No one but a lawyer could make the answer to a simple question so complicated, nor say it with a straight face. And she still didn't know what agency he was with.

"Does Lottie need a lawyer present?" Harve asked.

"That is her choice of course, but Ms. Carlyle is not now, nor can I conceive of any circumstances in the future whereby she would become, a suspect. I'd like to ask her some questions, but I am merely seeking information."

That at least was good news, Lottie thought. "Can Harve stay?" she asked.

"I have no objections," he said.

"So, what do you want to know, Mr. Ludlow?"

"Anything you can tell me, Ms. Carlyle, such as what originally made you suspicious and why."

Lottie explained that the interest postings on the investment account had caught her attention, and so she'd finally decided to look for the original investment-account documents and to check the earlier records.

"That was the day you were locked in the downstairs vault, is that correct?"

"Yes, that's right."

"Do you have any idea, any suspicions, about who might have done it?"

"No," she told him. "I thought I was alone in the bank when I went downstairs."

"And now you think there was someone else there?"

"Either that or someone came in after I was already downstairs."

"But who would know you were still in the bank?"

"Anyone might have suspected it, I suppose. My car was parked right out front."

"That's why I thought she might still be inside," Harve interrupted. "I couldn't find her anywhere in town, and her car was still parked in its regular spot."

"And who would have access to the bank af-ter-hours, Ms. Carlyle?"

"Technically only my uncle, Cyrus Blackburn, my cousin, Jefferson, and myself. But we're a small bank, Mr. Ludlow, almost like family. I don't think the alarm has been reprogrammed in years. Any employee might have the codes."

"Just like any employee might have computer access?"

"I'm afraid so."

"You didn't make any notes and leave them ly-ing around for someone else to read and discover what you were up to, did you?"

"No, of course not," Lottie said. "I kept a diary of sorts, but I had it with me all the time, even when I was in the vault."

"What do you mean, a diary of sorts, Ms. Car-lyle?" Ludlow asked in a monotone that betrayed no emotion.

"It's a chronological record, kind of a running commentary of what I suspected and what I did. I put it on a computer disk, not into the computer itself, and kept the disk locked in my briefcase. I made each entry a separate file, thinking that the computer recording of time and date saved would be some sort of documentation." She paused. "A dumb idea, huh?"

Ludlow straightened in his chair. "Not at all. Ac-tually it was a smart idea, assuming you didn't leave it lying around where someone could see it.

Do you—'' he cleared his throat ''—do you happen to still have it?''

''I have it right here,'' she told him, opening her briefcase. She withdrew the disk.

''Could I borrow this or maybe a copy?'' he asked.

''I can make you a copy,'' Harve told him. ''That will preserve the date and time coding. My computer's in my office.''

''All right. Thank you.'' Ludlow returned his attention to Lottie. ''Ms. Carlyle, may I ask how far back you checked the investment records?''

''I found the same pattern in place for approximately five years,'' she said.

''I see. And did you also examine even earlier records? Say those of approximately thirteen years ago?''

She nodded slowly. ''How did you know?''

''Under the circumstances and given the opportunity, I believe most people would have done the same thing,'' he said. ''Tell me, what did you find?''

''The same investment pattern.''

''And what did you conclude?''

''That a copycat embezzler was at work.''

''Or...'' he prompted.

''Or that the original embezzler was at work again.'' She heard Harve's indrawn breath, but didn't dare turn to look at him, afraid she'd lose her composure.

"My experts tell me that the pattern is almost too exact for a copycat," Ludlow said softly.

"You mean..."

"It's still early in the investigation," he said, "but at the moment we suspect we're dealing with a repeat embezzler. It appears your father may not have been guilty of the earlier embezzlement, after all. And that, Ms. Carlyle, also raises the question of your father's manner of death. At this late date we may never know for sure if it was suicide, an accident or murder. Any of the three are possibilities."

Lottie closed her eyes briefly, digesting the investigator's words. Then he continued, "Embezzlement is usually a nonviolent white-collar crime," he continued. "But this case doesn't seem usual. I hope I don't have to tell you to report anything suspicious, anything that seems out of the ordinary, to us immediately."

"I will," she said.

"And you'll be extremely careful?"

"Yes," she promised.

"All right, then, if Mr. Tremayne will make me a copy of that disk, I'll get out of here."

After he'd made the copy and seen Ludlow off, Harve asked Lottie, "Why didn't you tell me about your father?"

"I was afraid," she said.

"Afraid?"

"I wanted, no, *want* it to be true so much I guess

I was afraid to hope. It seems impossible after all this time. I think I was afraid I was fooling myself. What if it turns out to be a copycat, after all?''

"Then nothing's changed," he reminded her. "Not worse, not better, simply the same. And you've learned to live with that. Right?"

"Right," she said, her voice trembling.

"Lottie, sweetheart, come here." And he folded her into his arms.

# CHAPTER SIXTEEN

THE HOT SPELL continued. The bank examiners left shortly after noon Friday without making an official announcement of their findings. It might have been better if they had, Lottie thought. Rumors and speculation spread through the bank and the town with the speed of a hound on a blood scent.

They'd be looking for the money now, she realized, checking for unexpected resources, expensive purchases and investments beyond the means of declared incomes.

The money her father was accused of taking had never been found. Her grandfather Blackburn had repaid the bank from his own private funds, an action that had only reinforced the breach between her mother and the rest of the family. Sarah had claimed it was an admission that the family believed William was guilty, which, of course, they did. The rift had never been mended.

Lottie had returned to Little Falls, hoping to heal the family wounds as much as she'd hoped to save the bank. She realized now that it wasn't going to happen. If anything, the rift in the family was even greater.

She'd welcomed the growing friendship and familial connection she'd found with Jeannie. But now Jeff was barely speaking to her and, as his wife, Jeannie would follow his lead.

Lottie's return had resurrected old hurts, old crimes and new guilt. Even though she was just the catalyst for discovery, she'd be blamed, if only for acting as messenger. The ugliness set in motion by her return would not be easily forgotten. Or forgiven.

But the worst, the absolutely worst thing she'd done, was fall in love with Harve Tremayne.

She'd left him with no doubt she loved him. And he'd left her with no doubt he didn't return that love.

Even when he'd comforted her last night, he'd treated her as a dear friend or maybe a beloved younger sister.

That wasn't enough.

She'd had no control over much of the pain she'd experienced in her life, but she did have control over this. She couldn't, wouldn't, live in the same town with him, seeing him every day, loving him the way she did, not when she knew he didn't return that love.

As soon as the problems at the bank were resolved, she would rent her house or sell it or maybe turn it over to the historical society on a long-term lease, then leave and start a new life somewhere else. It was the only thing she could do.

Harve called shortly after noon to tell her he might be a few minutes late meeting her after work.

"Don't stay in the bank alone," he said. "And don't leave town until I get there. Stay around other people. Why don't you wait at the Down Home?"

Much as she'd like to see Myrtle, she was still reluctant to go to the Down Home. "I'll drive over to my house, instead," she told him. "I need to check on the repairs, anyway. It's only a few blocks, and the contractor will be there. I won't be alone."

He protested at first, then finally agreed after again warning her to be careful.

As Lottie left the bank, the heat rolled over her in waves, almost stealing her breath. She started the engine of her car, turned the air conditioner on, then stepped out of the car and closed the door, waiting for the interior to cool. She glanced up and down Main Street. No pedestrians today, for anyone with any sense was indoors. And most of them would be sitting in front of a blowing fan, sipping a glass of iced tea.

She waited another couple of minutes before opening the car door and getting in. It was still hot, but marginally cooler than the outside temperature, and the air conditioner was blowing valiantly.

Lottie had driven half a block past the section of the highway known as Main Street when she saw Emma Whitehall walking slowly along the side of the road, her face red, either from the effort of walking or the heat or both.

Impulsively Lottie pulled over. Emma wasn't her favorite person, but she couldn't drive by and do nothing. The woman looked as if she was about to suffer a heatstroke.

Leaning across to the passenger seat, Lottie rolled down the window. "Emma, what are you doing out in this furnace?"

"Walking home. My car's in the garage."

"Get in and I'll drive you home. It's too hot to be walking."

The woman hesitated a moment, seeming to look around to see if anyone else would offer her a ride before accepting. Finally she opened the car door and settled herself in the passenger seat.

"Roll up the window," Lottie told her. "I've got the air-conditioning on."

"My car doesn't have air-conditioning," Emma said in a voice that sounded almost bitter.

"It's nice to have, especially on days like this." Lottie kept her voice as pleasant as possible. The last thing she wanted today was a confrontation with Emma. If she remembered correctly, Emma's house was only about a half a mile down the highway, on a side street. Surely she could keep the peace for that short a distance.

Emma fastened her seat belt and said nothing, but Lottie noticed the color in her face returning to normal.

"Is the next turnoff yours?" she asked, more for confirmation than information.

"Just stay on the highway."

She glanced at Emma. "But I thought—" She

stopped cold when she saw the wicked-looking little gun in Emma's hand.

"What...what are you doing?"

"Everything was going to be fine," Emma said in a conversational voice. "Then you came back and spoiled it all. So now I'm going to make you pay."

Lottie glanced in her rearview mirror, hoping against hope she'd see Harve's green truck behind her. The road was empty.

"So you're the one stealing from the bank," Lottie said, struggling to keep her voice as matter-of-fact as Emma's.

"I'm not stealing. It's mine."

"It's called embezzlement, Emma, and you know it."

"Take the next left turn off the highway."

"It won't work, Emma. I'm supposed to be meeting Harve now. When I don't arrive, he'll come looking for me."

"No one saw you pick me up. He won't know where to find you. Not for a while. Turn here," she ordered again.

"Where—" Lottie's voice caught in her throat. She swallowed and tried again. "Where are we going?"

"Why, to the lake bluff of course. When they do find you, it'll be exactly where they found your father. Poor girl, they'll say. Such a sad ending, but you know, bad blood will out. Like father, like daughter.''

And then Emma laughed.

WHERE WAS LOTTIE?

Harve drove down Main Street for the second time, fighting to control his growing anxiety. When he'd arrived at her house, there was no sign of her. The contractor reported he hadn't seen her.

Her car wasn't parked at the bank, either.

He'd had a bad feeling about her idea to meet him at her house. He should have heeded his intuition. Should have insisted she stay in town. But it was only a few blocks from the bank to her house, and she'd convinced him she'd be safe.

His fault. He should have known better.

He tried dialing her car phone. No answer. Did she have it turned off? Probably.

*Stay calm,* he told himself. He knew she usually didn't turn on the car phone. But if she was in trouble, wouldn't she call him? Of course—if she could.

He made another sweep of the downtown area.

No red car. No Lottie.

Could he have missed her heading out of town?

On impulse he turned into Clyde's.

''Yeah, I saw her car go by a few minutes ago,'' Clyde told him. ''She pulled off to the side of the road about a block up the highway. Looked like she was picking up Ms. Emma. You know, Emma Whitehall, the lady that works at the bank. I think she was offering her a ride. It's too hot a day for an old lady to be walking. I'd have given her a ride myself if I'd seen her. But I didn't until I saw Ms. Carlyle stop.''

Harve felt a surge of relief. Maybe that was how he'd missed her. If he'd been driving by at the same time she'd turned off the highway to drop Emma at her house, he wouldn't have seen her.

Lottie was probably at her house by now waiting for him.

He headed back to the house, hoping he was right. But Lottie wasn't there. And again the contractor reported he hadn't seen her. Harve's growing concern was eating a hole in his belly.

Dammit. Where *was* she?

Again he told himself to stay calm. Maybe she'd stopped at Emma's for a few minutes. Maybe she was still there.

Okay, he'd go to Emma's. If she wasn't there, maybe Emma would know where she was.

He pulled back onto the highway, then turned off on the side street that led to Emma's house.

No red car in front.

He knocked on the door. No answer.

No Emma. No car. No Lottie.

What the hell was going on?

Was Emma still with her? Was Lottie taking Emma somewhere? Wouldn't she have called to let him know? She knew how worried he'd be when he couldn't find her. But where would she be going with Emma? From what Lottie had told him, she and the old lady got along like oil and water. Unless...unless...

*Dear God!*

He'd played the guessing game, trying to figure out the identity of the embezzler. He'd considered Cyrus and Jefferson, even Hiram, an antisocial type if he'd ever seen one. Never once had he considered Emma.

Why? Because she was a woman?

Or because she was an old lady, nearly ready for retirement. She'd worked at the bank for years—*years*—long before William Carlyle's time. Regardless of her title, she'd been Cyrus's secretary, assistant and confidant. She knew the bank. She knew the system. She could very well be the embezzler.

And he'd never given her more than a passing thought.

Now Lottie was with Emma, maybe against her will.

*Oh, Lottie, what have you gotten yourself into this time?*

He drove the highway slowly, looking for any sign to tell him where Lottie might have gone, looking for anyone who might have seen her.

He almost missed the two boys walking in the ditch along the side of the highway, fishing poles over their shoulders. He made a U-turn in the middle of the highway and pulled off the pavement beside them.

"Hey, guys," he called out the window, "I'm looking for a lady driving a red car. I was supposed to meet her, but I must've missed her. Either of you see a red car drive by in the last few minutes?''

"Yeah," the bigger of the two boys answered. "We saw a red car. It turned off the highway back there a ways. You know, the turnoff to the lake bluff?''

Harve's blood ran cold.

"THIS WON'T WORK, Emma. They know I'm not the embezzler," Lottie said. She'd followed Emma's instructions, turning off the highway as ordered. What she was driving on now was more path than road. The limbs of trees on both sides of the track almost met overhead. The front wheels wallowed in and out of a deep rut. She dropped the car into its lowest gear.

"Of course it'll work. You'll commit 'suicide,' just like your father. An admission of guilt. It worked before."

Lottie struggled to swallow the pain and anguish that this new knowledge of how her father had died brought. She took a deep, even breath and said, "But not this time, Emma. I've only been at the bank for a few months. They know the embezzlement's been taking place for several years. I can't be the thief.''

The car lurched from side to side. Emma lurched with it, bracing herself with one arm against the car door. The other hand still held the gun.

"It doesn't matter," she said. "You still have to pay.''

*Keep her talking,* Lottie told herself. *She's a crazy old woman. But even if you can't outthink her, maybe you can outrun her.*

"Why?" she asked. "What have I ever done to you? Why do *I* have to pay?"

"Your mother got to keep her bank stocks even after her husband stole from the bank. She kept her stocks and she left them to you. If they hadn't stolen *my* mother's stocks, she would have left them to me. Then I'd own part of the bank, too. I *should* own part of the bank. I only took what was mine."

"But my father didn't steal from the bank, did he, Emma? You did that. And my family didn't steal the stocks from your mother. Your father sold them. He didn't even sell them to my family. I've done nothing to harm you."

Emma didn't seem to hear. "You shouldn't have come back. I tried to get you to go away. You wouldn't listen."

"You locked me in the vault, didn't you?" Lottie accused.

Emma smirked. "Of course. If you didn't want anyone to know you were in the bank, you shouldn't have left your car parked right in front. I went in through the back door. The bank's doorlock codes haven't been changed since your father died."

"Did you sabotage my tire, too?"

"That was dead easy. I saw you go in the Down Home. My car was parked right next to yours. A woman who lives alone, even an old woman like me, knows how to remove a hubcap. It only took a moment. If anyone had seen me, I would have pretended I was checking my own tire."

Lottie swallowed. "So what do you want me to do now?"

"I told you. You have to die, like your father. Then everything will be all right. I'll retire next year, you know. I'll be sixty-five. Over forty years working at the bank. They'll probably give me a gold watch—a gold watch after forty years," she sneered. "Or a plaque. But that's all right. I knew they wouldn't take care of my retirement, so I've taken care of it myself."

*She really* is *crazy,* Lottie realized.

A small sapling was growing in the middle of the path, and Lottie steered to the side to avoid it. The car lurched again, the undercarriage hanging for a moment on a high rut. Emma's hand still held tight to the gun.

"Tell me, Emma. How did you kill my father?"

"Your father committed suicide."

"No, he didn't. You told me he didn't. Don't you remember?"

"I did?" The old woman looked puzzled for a minute. "Oh, well, I guess it doesn't matter now. I told William I had some information about the embezzlement. Told him to meet me here and I'd give it to him. Silly man. He thought I was harmless. It was easy. A little hit on the head with a rock, then I put the car in gear and gave it a push."

She shrugged. "By the time the car bounced

down the side of the bluff and landed in the water, one more bump on the head didn't make much difference.''

Lottie thought she might throw up, but fought it. She wasn't going to die the same way as her father, not if she could help it.

One wheel slipped into another rut, tilting the car crazily. She hung on to the steering wheel as the car righted itself. Then suddenly she was out of the woods and in the clearing at the top of the bluff. She could see the blue of the lake in the distance.

*Now or never!* Lottie hit the brakes, hard, and slammed the automatic gear into park. The sudden jolt threw Emma forward against the seat belt.

Lottie flung open her door, rolled out of the car and, scrambling to her feet, headed for the underbrush.

"Stop! Come back! Get in the car!" Emma shouted. "I'll shoot you."

Lottie ducked behind a tree. "Go ahead, Emma, shoot me," she called. "But I won't get back in the car. And if you shoot me, they'll know it wasn't suicide. Your plan won't work. Not this time."

"It will. It has to work. Come back. Right now." The old woman sounded close to tears.

"Give up, Emma. Put down the gun. It's over."

"No." She pointed the gun in Lottie's direction and pulled the trigger just as Harve's truck careered into the clearing.

Lottie heard the bullet whiz by her ear.

"No!" Emma cried again. She waved the gun in

the direction of the truck, then back toward Lottie's hiding place.

"Lottie, are you all right?" Harve yelled.

"Yes," she shouted back.

"Then stay where you are."

As if she could do anything else. She peeked around the tree, saw Harve open the door and step out of the truck.

*Be careful,* she said silently.

"Put down the gun, Emma." Harve took a step toward her. "I'm not going to hurt you."

Emma retreated a step. "No. Stay where you are."

He moved forward again. "Please, Emma. Put down the gun before someone gets hurt."

Emma swung the gun in Lottie's direction. "Don't come any closer. I'll shoot her. I will." She took another step backward and pointed the gun at Harve again.

Lottie held her breath.

"Stop, Emma," Harve called. "You're too close to the bluff."

"No. Stay away." She turned toward the tree that hid Lottie. "It's all your fault. You weren't supposed to come back. If you'd stayed away, everything would've been fine." She waved the gun at Harve and retreated another step.

Lottie saw the ground start to crumble under Emma's feet. Harve reached forward, trying to catch her.

He was too late.

Emma screamed once, her arms flailing the air. Then she disappeared.

Lottie ran toward Harve and threw herself at him. He caught her in his arms. "Are you all right?" he asked, his voice shaking. "Did she hurt you?"

"No, no. I'm okay."

He held her close. "Don't ever do that to me again," he said. "When I couldn't find you... I don't think I've ever been so afraid."

Lottie buried her face in his shoulder. "She killed my father, Harve. She told me. She was going to kill me, too. She said I'd look like a suicide, like Dad. Only I...only I wouldn't..."

"Wouldn't what, sweetheart?"

"I wouldn't let her. I told her...I told her if she wanted me dead, she'd have to shoot me. Then no one would believe it was a suicide and all her plans would go wrong."

"Shh. It's all right now. Everything's going to be all right."

Lottie took a deep breath and struggled to bring herself under control. "Is she...?"

"I don't know," he said. "I don't see how she could have survived the fall, but I'd better look." He led Lottie away from the edge of the bluff and back toward the center of the clearing. "Stay here," he told her.

"Be careful."

He smiled at her and walked back toward the edge, then lay down on his stomach and slowly inched forward. "I can see her," he said. "She's on the rocks. She's not moving." He worked his way back from the edge of the bluff and stood up. "I'll have to go down."

"Harve, no."

"I'll be fine. I've got rope in the truck. I'll make a harness and attach it to the bumper. Can you move your car around so I can get the truck a little closer to the edge? And have you got your cell phone?"

She nodded.

"Then call for help," he said. "Although I suspect it's too late."

Lottie moved like an automaton, following his instructions. She started the car and backed it to the side of the clearing. Harve moved the truck forward.

She called for assistance, telling the dispatcher that Emma had fallen over the cliff. Then she got out of the car to watch Harve.

He took two ropes from the back of the truck and tied them both to the front bumper, then fashioned one into a harness and stepped into it.

"I wish you'd wait," she told him.

"I'll be fine. I'll rappel down. If I get in trouble, the harness'll catch me. But stay away from the edge," he warned. "It's crumbling." Then he lowered himself over the side and disappeared from sight.

She was watching the place she last saw him when the emergency crew, led by Isaac Easton, arrived. "Who's down there? Harve?"

Lottie nodded.

The chief lay down on his belly the same way Harve had earlier and worked his way to the edge of the bluff, then, a moment later wriggled back. "No need to hurry," he told the crew. "I think we can reach them easier by water. Harve signaled he'd stay with the...with her."

Police Chief Billy Bob Simpson arrived moments later, siren blaring, although the car was moving at a snail's pace. She was surprised, however, when Investigator Ludlow stepped from the passenger side of the squad car.

"Are you all right, Ms. Carlyle?" he asked.

She nodded, afraid to trust her voice.

"I'm sorry we didn't move a little faster. If we had, it would've saved you a bad time."

"You...you knew it was Emma?"

"We were reasonably sure. In fact, we were on our way to talk to her when your call came in."

"She did it. She admitted it to me. And...and she killed my father."

Ludlow cleared his throat. "I'm sorry," he said. "Look, Ms. Carlyle, I'm going to need a statement, but I think we can find somewhere more comfortable than this. Is that your car?"

She nodded again.

"Then why don't I drive you back to town? I'd consider it a favor. I don't want a return trip under siren, and I suspect that's exactly what your police chief will do."

"But Harve..."

"Don't worry. They're going to pick them up by boat. It'll be safer than trying to bring them back up the cliff. But it'll take a while. I think they're launching the boat from somewhere near Springdale."

She sighed. "Then I'd appreciate your driving me back to town. I'm not sure I can."

The next two hours passed in a blur. Lottie gave Ludlow her statement, repeating everything she could remember Emma telling her. Then she'd waited while it was typed, read it for accuracy and signed it.

She wasn't sure where Harve was. She did know he was safe. Ludlow told her when the boat, carrying Harve and Emma's body, returned to the marina.

After assuring the inspector she felt well enough to drive, she said goodbye and walked to her car.

It was over, she thought as she sat in her car wondering what to do. She couldn't go to the farm. Harve wouldn't be there and Annie would have already gone home. She didn't want to go to Abby's. Abigail would welcome her, but...well, she didn't feel up to talking.

She'd go to her house, she decided. There was no reason to be afraid of being alone now. She was safe. The bank was safe. Recovery of the funds Emma had embezzled and socked away for retirement would put it on a firm financial footing. And she'd cleared her father's name. She'd done everything she'd set out to do. And more. It was finally over.

What was she going to do with the rest of her life?

HARVE FOUND HER at her house a couple of hours later, asleep in the front-porch swing, her bare feet curled under her like a child's.

She was wearing a pair of faded denim shorts and an oversize plaid shirt, open at the collar, sleeves raggedly cut off at the elbow. The sun had slipped below the horizon only moments ago, and in the lingering twilight he could see tendrils of her dark hair curling damply along the nape of her neck. Her eyelashes formed dark crescents against her flushed cheeks.

He'd never seen her look more beautiful.

Why had she come here and not gone to his farm or his grandmother's to wait for him?

He wanted to pick her up in his arms, needing to feel her, needing to reassure himself she was alive and well.

Instead, he sank onto the porch, leaned back against one of the porch columns and told himself, now that he'd found her, now that he could see her, he was content to wait.

The smell of stale smoke still lingered faintly in the air, reminding him again of how close he'd come to losing her. But the danger, the threats, were finally over. She was safe.

She stirred in her sleep and set the swing to

gently rocking. She moved again, then stretched, blinking her eyes.

He remained where he was, watching her, trying not to move, not wanting to startle her.

She returned to awareness by degrees, looking around as if becoming conscious of her surroundings. At last her gaze rested on him.

"Harve?" she asked, her voice low and hesitant, unsure.

"Ah, so you're awake now," he murmured, and got to his feet.

"What are you doing here?" she asked. "Are you all right?"

"I'm fine," he told her. "And that's a question I should be asking you. As for what I'm doing here, where else would I be except with you?"

She shook her head, as if still trying to clear her thoughts. "Emma?"

"Emma's dead, Lottie," he said. "It's all over."

He took a step toward her and she shifted in the swing seat. He wasn't sure whether it was her intention to make room for him or to put distance between them. He didn't ask. Instead, taking advantage of the space beside her, he sat down.

She looked at him, then at her hands, twisting them in her lap. "I've decided to sell the house," she said calmly, as if she was telling him the time of day.

"If that's what you want," he replied. "It's a beautiful old house, though. I thought you might want to keep it in the family—you know, maybe just rent it out—in case one of our children some-day wants to—''

"Children?''

"Don't you want children, Lottie? I just thought… But there's time to talk about that later. It's your house. If you want to sell it, that's your decision. Whatever you decide is fine with me.''

"But I…you…''

"But what? You *are* going to marry me, aren't you?''

"Marry you? You don't love me.''

"Not love you?''

His stomach churned and his mind reeled. How could she not know he loved her? He struggled to keep his voice under control.

"Not love you?'' he repeated. "I only love you a little more than the air I breathe. Dear Lord, Lot-tie, how could you think I don't love you? How could you not know?''

"The last week…at the farm…you didn't so much as kiss me.''

"I didn't dare. If I'd kissed you, it wouldn't have stopped with a kiss. I told Chief Easton I was keep-ing you at the farm to protect you. I told Annie and my grandmother the same thing. I didn't want to take advantage of the situation and I didn't trust myself…. The last five nights have been the longest of my life. I don't know how much longer I could have continued to see you, be with you and not… Never believe I don't love you, Lottie. Love you and want you. You have to marry me.''

His breath ran out with a shudder. "I'm doing it again, aren't I? Ordering you around. I haven't even asked you to marry me, have I?"

She shook her head.

He took her hands, holding them in his as if clutching a lifeline. "Will you marry me, Lottie? Will you love me and live with me? Will you be the sunlight and laughter in my days, the solace and comfort in my nights? Will you be my strength, my companion, the mother of my children? For as long as we both shall live?"

"Yes."

Her eyes were wide and luminous, and there was a spark of laughter deep in their emerald depths.

"Did you say yes?"

"Yes," she repeated. "I said yes."

He pulled her to him fiercely. Then he kissed her.

It was a kiss of joy and promise, of thankfulness, a kiss for a tired soul to melt into.

Finally he raised his mouth from hers and, still holding her close, pushed against the porch floor with his foot.

The swing swayed in response.

"When?" he asked. "When will you marry me? Would Thursday be too soon? We can get the license Monday. The three-day waiting period would be up Thursday. Unless you want a big wedding?"

"Not particularly, but your grandmother might."

"My grandmother will be so delighted I'm marrying you she'd rush us off tonight if she could," he said. "We'll put her in charge of planning a reception. She and Annie. Say in about six weeks. That'll give them time to plan the biggest wedding reception Little Falls has ever seen. So, will you marry me Thursday?''

She'd come to Little Falls to rescue the bank and start a new life. She'd never dreamed she'd be able to lift the shadow from her past, to redeem her father's honor and lay him to rest.

And she'd certainly never dreamed she'd find the love of her life.

"Yes, Harve," she said. "I'll marry you Thursday."

"Thank you, Lord," he said, his eyes raised toward the heavens. Then he stood, pulled her gently to her feet and murmured softly, "Let's go home."

She was more than happy to comply.

**HARLEQUIN SUPERROMANCE®**

*Loving*
**DANGEROUSLY**

They're tall, dark and dangerous. Exciting. The kind of men who give women thrills—and chills. The women are daring, strong, compassionate—and willing to take a risk. Danger may threaten, but together the hero and heroine can face any challenges. Even the challenge of love.

Look for these upcoming *Loving Dangerously* books:

Available wherever Harlequin books are sold.

Cupid's going undercover
this Valentine's Day in

# The Cupid Connection

Cupid has his work
cut out for him this
Valentine's Day with these
three stories about three
couples who are just too *busy*
to fall in love...well, not for long!

**ONE MORE VALENTINE**
by Anne Stuart
**BE MINE, VALENTINE**
by Vicki Lewis Thompson
**BABY ON THE DOORSTEP**
by Kathy Gillen Thacker

Make the Cupid Connection this February 1998!

Available wherever Harlequin and Silhouette books are sold.

HARLEQUIN®   Silhouette®

# WELCOME TO *Love Inspired* ™

## A brand-new series of contemporary inspirational love stories.

Join men and women as they learn valuable lessons about facing the challenges of today's world and about life, love and faith.

Look for the following February 1998
Love Inspired™ titles:

*A Groom of Her Own*
by Irene Hannon

*The Marriage Wish*
by Dee Henderson

*The Reluctant Bride*
by Kathryn Alexander

Available in retail outlets
in January 1998.

**LIFT YOUR SPIRITS AND GLADDEN YOUR
HEART with *Love Inspired* ™!**

Steeple
Hill™

LI298

**Make a Valentine's date
for the premiere of**
◈ HARLEQUIN® **Movies**
**starting February 14, 1998 with**

# Debbie Macomber's
# This Matter of
# Marriage

on **the movie channel** tmc

Just tune in to **The Movie Channel** the **second Saturday night** of every month at 9:00 p.m. EST to join us, and be swept away by the sheer thrill of romance brought to life. Watch for details of upcoming movies—in books, in your television viewing guide and in stores.

If you are not currently a subscriber to The Movie Channel, simply call your local cable or satellite provider for more details. Call today, and don't miss out on the romance!

**the movie channel** tmc
*100% pure movies.
100% pure fun.*

◈ HARLEQUIN™
*Makes any time special.*™

# Don't miss these Harlequin favorites by some of our top-selling authors!

| | | | |
|---|---|---|---|
| HT#25733 | THE GETAWAY BRIDE | $3.50 U.S. | ☐ |
| | by Gina Wilkins | $3.99 CAN. | ☐ |
| HP#11849 | A KISS TO REMEMBER | $3.50 U.S. | ☐ |
| | by Miranda Lee | $3.99 CAN. | ☐ |
| HR#03431 | BRINGING UP BABIES | $3.25 U.S. | ☐ |
| | by Emma Goldrick | $3.75 CAN. | ☐ |
| HS#70723 | SIDE EFFECTS | $3.99 U.S. | ☐ |
| | by Bobby Hutchinson | $4.50 CAN. | ☐ |
| HI#22377 | CISCO'S WOMAN | $3.75 U.S. | ☐ |
| | by Aimée Thurlo | $4.25 CAN. | ☐ |
| HAR#16666 | ELISE & THE HOTSHOT LAWYER | $3.75 U.S. | ☐ |
| | by Emily Dalton | $4.25 CAN. | ☐ |
| HH#28949 | RAVEN'S VOW | $4.99 U.S. | ☐ |
| | by Gayle Wilson | $5.99 CAN. | ☐ |

**(limited quantities available on certain titles)**

| | |
|---|---|
| AMOUNT | $ _____ |
| POSTAGE & HANDLING | $ _____ |
| ($1.00 for one book, 50¢ for each additional) | |
| APPLICABLE TAXES* | $ _____ |
| TOTAL PAYABLE | $ _____ |

(check or money order—please do not send cash)

To order, complete this form and send it, along with a check or money order for the total above, payable to Harlequin Books, to: **In the U.S.**: 3010 Walden Avenue, P.O. Box 9047, Buffalo, NY 14269-9047; **In Canada**: P.O. Box 613, Fort Erie, Ontario, L2A 5X3.

Name: _____

Address: _____ City: _____

State/Prov.: _____ Zip/Postal Code: _____

Account Number (if applicable): _____

*New York residents remit applicable sales taxes.
Canadian residents remit applicable GST and provincial taxes.

Look us up on-line at: http://www.romance.net

075-CSAS

HBLJM98